MW00784910

COLLAPSE: Ashfall Apocalypse 2

An Apocalyptic Thriller

M.L. Banner

Toes in the Water Publishing, LLC

Copyright © 2022 by Michael L. Banner
All rights reserved.

ISBN: (Paperback): 978-1-947510-11-1

ISBN: (eBook): 978-1-947510-10-4

COLLAPSE: ASHFALL APOCALYPSE 2 is an original work of fiction.

The characters and dialogs are the products of this author's vivid imagination.

Much of the science and the historical incidents described in this novel are based on reality, as are its warnings.

No portion of this book may be reproduced in any form without written permission from the publisher or author, except as permitted by U.S. copyright law.

PROLOGUE

Leticia - Recording Labeled "Buster"

I confess that the man others jokingly referred to as Buster because of a flatulence problem, who was the son of Polar Bear—the leader of a vast drug cartel—was the same person who had killed my parents, in front of me, because of my actions, and then left me to freeze to death. Also, I confess that I couldn't help myself.

You see, I wanted him dead. So when his gaudy golden gun dropped in front of me, without thinking, I picked it up and I shot him. Then I shot him again. And again. And with each pull of the trigger of this disgusting man's gun, I kept my eyes closed while I pictured his face the day that he shot my father and then my mother, with the same gun. I pictured how he smiled at me, with murder in his eyes, knowing that I was the one who would suffer, instead of him...

And when I was the one on the opposite end of the gun, I know I was smiling right back at him, as I pounded one lead bullet after another into him, until his heavy gun stopped firing.

All I could hear was a dull ring in my head and the thump-thump sounds of my heart attempting to break through my ribcage.

When I chanced a glance at his body—

❄ ❄ ❄

There was a noise, so I clicked off the recorder.

As rapidly as I could, I snatched out the SD card and scribbled on it, "Buster." This went immediately into a baggie, which then found its way deep in the recesses of my black satchel, with the other cards. In hindsight, I guess I should have taken better care of them.

Anyway, I leapt out of my chair, and bounded out the room.

Once again, my heart threatened to break my ribs...

ENTRANCE INTERVIEW - PART 2

SUBJECTS: R. Ash, N. Thompson & L. Brown

For the record, I am introducing multiple sources of the story of R. Ash, N. Thompson & L. Brown, to better make sense of what happened to them and how they came to find us.

I'm also adding into the record all other relevant interviews which help us better understand their story, including audio recordings and other transcripts in their chronological order,

to give the best representation of their story.

It is on this basis that I have entered into the record what follows.

- HL

CHAPTER 1

Ron

The moment I spotted the man, I knew one of us was going to die.

He had marched up from the rear river path, bisecting my vacant house's yard and the contiguous home we were all living in. The man approached hunched over. His head was crooked upward, and his steps were controlled, telegraphing only part of his intentions. The sledgehammer in one hand and the dark semi-auto pistol in the other told me the rest: He was here to break into our house, steal from us and, and if we stood in his way, he would murder us.

If I didn't stop him first.

I inched a little closer, doing my utmost to remain hidden from him, while at the same time getting a better position. He was less than fifty yards from me now.

Easy shot, assuming he was alone.

Since his hands were already occupied, I was guessing there had to be at least one other, waiting for this lead intruder to find a way in. Unfortunately, that meant I couldn't just shoot this man while my people were so exposed, and I didn't know where the other intruders were. The report from my weapon, even though it was suppressed, would be too loud.

Dammit! I cursed myself for not carrying a radio with me so I could easily warn them. I'd only intended to be gone for a few minutes—just enough time to grab a small part from my workshop next door, and then check on our hydro-power generator and clear away any debris. Ten or fifteen minutes max. Not enough time to warrant being tied to some damned radio. Or so I thought.

At least I brought my rifle.

The intruder halted beside the thick oak that I had carved in Liz's and my initials so long ago. His hammer hand covered my juvenile show of affection, while he squirreled his head around its trunk to gaze upon our newly created greenhouse, just a few feet away from him.

From my position at the back edge of my own house, I could plainly see the illuminated silhouettes of Nanette and Chloe, working away. Their forms were obvious without their bulky clothing. As expected, neither Joey, Leticia or Dog were visible: I had just left them downstairs, telling them I'd return in a few minutes.

The intruder bear-hugged the tree and craned his neck farther out to get a better look at Nanette and Chloe. He was clearly taking longer than he needed to case the rear of our house and find a way to force his way in. Then I realized what he was doing: He was leering at the women.

Rage ignited inside of me, not just because of this man's intentions, but because of my stupidity at leaving the greenhouse so unprotected.

Although Buster and his gang were no longer a threat, that didn't mean the rest of the world would leave us alone. We had all been lulled into a sense of normalcy once again, because we hadn't seen anyone for weeks... except for a small convoy of trucks passing in the distance yesterday.

And now, looking at this harsh reality, I could see all that it would take to break into the greenhouse was a sharp knife to pierce the two layers of plastic. The house it was connected to was protected with rolling shutters which blocked the three entrances. Yet, as long as someone was in the greenhouse, the back door remained unshuttered. It was just plain foolhardy on my part to leave this part of the house so unprotected.

That was an issue for later.

Right now, I had to focus with all my might, to not act impatient or rash. I had to find out where the other intruder or intruders were first.

The back of my neck prickled at this thought, and I swiveled around, scanning the rear of both properties. I attempted to quiet my breaths with long inhales and exhales. Except for a light breeze, the world around me was silent, white and cold, like death. If there were others around, they weren't moving or they were too far away for me to hear them.

Rather abruptly, as if the intruder had just remembered his mission, he popped away from the tree and the greenhouse and beat a path forward in the deep snow, toward the street-side of the home.

I needed to get in front of the guy, while still being unseen by him or any of his buddies.

A quick turn and I darted for the other side, using the back of my house as cover. I carried my rifle up at a high port, conscious of the added barrel length from the suppressor—part of the supplies we'd procured from Buster's gang. My black flagpole of death made me stick out like a sore thumb against the thick covering of white snow on top of gray ash. But it was better than jamming the barrel into a berm and clogging it.

Fueling my anxiety even more was another colossal screw-up.

I had left the front door shutter unlocked. And if this intruder or one of his friends got there before me, it would be easy to get through the front door with one or two strikes of a sledgehammer, like the one in the intruder's hand. I had to get there before him.

As I rounded the front corner of my house, I halted when the man was visible.

The man had trudged through the cold slog of snow and ice, past the garage door, and stopped at its edge, where he peeked around to the front of the home. Was he looking for his other men, or just checking to see that there was no one around to interrupt his breaking and entering?

He appeared to have decided on his course of action, because he immediately spun and doubled back to the rear of the home. Now running, he was returning to the least protected area of our home, the greenhouse.

I no longer cared about remaining unseen or unheard: I double-timed it, at a diagonal, to where he was headed, hoping to cut him off before he reached his destination. My preference was to not kill the man. I'd done too much of this lately. I'd rather find out why he was snooping around our property and if anyone had sent him.

Deep down I knew, like when a dreadful cold seeps into your bones, I was going to have to shoot him.

Something cracked under my boot, and the man's head snapped toward me.

Shit.

He dropped his sledgehammer, while lifting his pistol in front of him, not breaking his stride. I took a knee, while taking aim at him with my rifle.

There was barely one hundred feet between us. Very easy shot for me, not as easy for him with a pistol. But like I said, I didn't want to shoot the guy, so I held my left hand up, sticking my palm out, while still keeping my sight trained on his chest and my right finger on the trigger.

The man halted and began to swing his pistol around toward me.

"Freeze," I demanded.

He did.

Then he took his eyes off me and looked around, as if he were trying to find something... or someone.

He's definitely not alone.

I gave a quick glance from side to side, while attempting to listen for any sounds of another person. Especially behind me. My neck prickled more at the thought that someone was watching me.

But there was no one else, at least that I could see or hear. Just the wind blowing and my heavy breathing.

The intruder and I returned our glares to each other, but he didn't move his pistol, which was still pointed at the ground, away from me.

I started to rise back up to a standing position, intending to continue to walk in his direction. To talk to him.

A scream pulled at both of us.

Based on the higher pitch, I knew it was Chloe.

The man swung his head back toward me. His pistol followed.

He pulled his trigger, and so did I.

❄ ❄ ❄

Nan

We were completely oblivious.

It was a long thin protrusion that stuck out of the plastic barrier between us and the outside, about shoulder high. It held there, unmoving, like some pointy brace in the wall which I had never noticed.

My brain second-guessed this, reasoning that maybe it was a branch from a nearby tree that had breached the plastic barrier and now was working its way in. And upward... But it was way too thin. Is it a knife blade?

Chloe had her back to this foreign object, her feet carefully planted in the middle of the lines of our green beans. She looked up and tossed me a questioning glance.

I didn't even acknowledge her. I kept my eyes drilled at this peculiar thing, trying to make sense of it for any further movement to confirm for me what I was seeing.

The protrusion then zipped downward in one fluid and rapid movement. It was like a slap across my face, as I knew with certainty it was a knife. Someone was coming in and I didn't have my gun with me.

I hesitated, just long enough for me to react. “Chloe, run!" I yelled. At the very same moment, I took off through the back door to go grab my gun. I heard her scream as I turned into the kitchen and bee-lined it to the table, on which rested our weapons.

By the time I returned to the doorway entrance into the greenhouse, my .357 in hand, a rough-looking man dressed in some quasi-military uniform had Chloe at knifepoint. Her eyes were wide and her face rigid. The man smiled through his grimy beard.

"Drop the knife, dirt-bag, or I'll drop you!" I said this with such certainty I almost believed it myself. My heart pumped adrenalin like a fire hose, but my hand held steady. I pulled back the hammer, to punctuate my resolve, the pistol clicking its acknowledgment that we were both ready.

There were muffled pops outside, like gunfire, that made me jump.

I glanced to my right, in their direction, then back at the man. He ignored me and glowered at Chloe, while licking his chops. Chloe tried unsuccessfully to slither away, but the man held tight with one claw around her bare abdomen.

In the midst of my gasping at this, Dog burst past me, almost knocking me down. Like a high-speed train, tracking directly at the man, Dog leapt at the man's knife arm.

The man looked up right when Dog struck, tearing the man's arm away from Chloe just long enough that she could get free.

Dog's locomotive power and weight knocked the man down onto his back, while Dog buried his canines into the man's arm. But rather than screaming in terror, like I would have done, the man did something I did not expect.

He reached around with his free hand, grabbing the knife out of the one being violently yanked about and swung the knife around at Dog.

Boom! sounded right beside me.

Boom-boom!

Many moments after the gun shots, I shook my head and slapped at my left ear. My eardrum felt like it had burst, and that side was deaf.

Joey stepped past me, his pistol extended outward, finger on the trigger, ready to fire again. But the man had given up the fight. Only his arm moved.

"Out, Dog," Joey hollered, as he marched closer to the fallen invader.

Dog dutifully opened his mouth and the invader's bloody limb slipped out, flopping onto two new sprouts of lettuce. The invader looked dead.

"Good Dog," Joey praised him, removing the hand he used to steady his gun to pet Dog, who happily accepted the compliment for a job well done.

Like that, the incident was over. And I had done nothing.

Chloe had been backing away the whole time, and now dashed around the rest of our garden and the fallen man. When she reached me, she threw her arms around me and sobbed. She seemed smaller than I had thought.

Time sort of halted, while I glared at the top of her petite head, and I felt her tears and sweat drip down the front of my sleeveless T.

I couldn't help but think what a strange life I now occupied: I had been beaten and raped so violently that I almost died, all perpetrated by my ex-husband, whom I later killed. And now, the mistress of my dead husband, whom I had caught bare-assed with him, was part of my new family, living with me and others in this home. And to top it off, she was seeking comfort from me, even though I too felt like my own basket case. I was barely hanging on by one dirty fingernail in this post-apocalyptic world in which we had to carry our guns everywhere, because at any moment another murderer was likely to show up at our door... or through our walls. I was so caught up with my own mix of wanting to cry with Chloe, or laugh hysterically, or both, I zoned out everything.

Then, adding to the surreal nature of it all, Ron's disembodied head popped through the cut in the plastic. He glanced first at the dead man, then at Joey and Dog, and then us. "You all right?" he whispered.

"We're fine," Joey answered. "Any others?"

"Yeah. One other. I dropped him. Going to search the perimeter. Just wanted to make sure you were all okay."

He glanced directly at me this time, looking for confirmation. I nodded.

But I wasn't too sure any of us were all right. In fact, I was quite sure we were not.

CHAPTER 2

Nan

"Doesn't this guy look like a hitman to you?" Ron whispered, forgetting I was right behind him, listening. From a knee, he pointed to a tattoo on the dead guy's cheek. It was three vertical slashes, like a rough Roman numeral three carved with a rusty knife.

"Not sure I know what a hitman looks like," Joey answered, standing over the body with his back to me. "That could have been a prison tattoo. See, it's somewhat jagged-looking."

Although my left ear rang like church bells on Sunday —preferable to hearing nothing out of that ear earlier —I could hear what they were saying well enough.

Ron tossed Joey a nod at that comment, and then shuddered when he saw me listening intently. He cleared his throat—an overt sign to cease talking about this. Obviously, Ron thought I needed to be protected from even the thought that this man had been a killer or in prison, as if these thoughts were too disturbing for my tender ears... It was just like my dead ex Bud used to act.

Joey seemed to acknowledge this concern by ending his hitman questions and returning to checking the dead man's pants pockets, then his white and gray winter coat.

Both men stayed clear of the blood pool, still growing by trickles from his Dog-mangled arm and gunshot wounds.

Dog lay close by in a corner of the room, resolute looking, resting against a dirt pile. His ears were on alert for the next bad guy who might offer him another chew-toy opportunity.

In spite of the attack and the hitman conversation, I felt... okay. Yes, I was over it. They didn't have to worry about their conversation affecting me. I wanted to tell them, Geez guys, I killed my ex after being brutally attacked. I can handle this stuff. No problem.

But I held back. And at that moment, my mind filled with the image of Bud's dead face. He looked just like this man: all the life strangled out of him.

I shook my head to clear out the image and focus on what Ron and Joey were saying.

"The guy doesn't have any ID on him," Ron said.

"What about the other one?" Joey motioned to the body they had dragged to just outside, where this intruder had come in.

"No, I already checked."

I wasn't sure any of us carried ID anymore, but whether they did or didn't wasn't what gnawed at my gut. And because neither of them asked the sixty-four-thousand-dollar-question out loud, I did. "Could these two be Buster's men?"

I expected a reflexive, 'No!' from Ron, but when he didn't answer, I felt my pulse ratchet up multiple beats.

Finally, Ron responded. "Don't think so. But..." He rose, his hands on his hips, his gaze falling from my eyes to my knees.

Ron and I weren't physically intimate, though I felt an emotional intimacy with him that I never had with Bud, or any other man. At least I thought I did. This of course was born out of going through hell and back with someone. After doing so, you pick up quickly on some of that person's habits and mannerisms. And although he had been more distant lately, I could tell that Ronald Ash was trying to soften what he was about to tell me, or perhaps tell all of us. But it was that protective thing men did that was so annoyingly macho. It shouldn't have bothered me, but it did.

"I should have said something yesterday, but I didn't want to spoil the day."

Chloe's grip on my arm tightened to the point of being painful. And when I reached over with a hand to comfort her—and loosen her grasp—I noticed Leticia's shadow in the greenhouse entry.

"Hang on," I said to Ron, and then turned to Chloe. "Thought you were going to keep her away from this?" I motioned with my head at the dead body.

Her eyes sparked with a flash of anger, her full lips pursed up, and then released their façade. She let her head drop and mumbled, "Just wanted to know who they were."

"Please take Leticia inside, and I'll come in and update you both," Joey pleaded.

She cast a sidelong glance through her disheveled hair at Joey, and then me, before letting her head drop again. "Fine!"

She then turned to the doorway and stomped out, gathering Leticia with one arm and closing the door behind them.

Slowly, I returned my gaze to Ron. "Okay, Ron. What did you see yesterday?"

I really didn't want to know.

"Was it that convoy of Humvees?" Joey asked.

Ron cocked his head and scowled, as if Joey had just revealed the very secret they'd both been hiding from us little women.

"What convoy of Humvees?" I asked, genuinely unaware.

Again, Ron's dark eyes darted down and then back up to me. "In the distance, while we were enjoying that brief moment of sunlight yesterday, I caught a glimpse of a convoy of Hummer trucks. They looked like... like they were going to Buster's compound. I thought it might have been the military... But I wasn't sure. They knew where they were going... Ah shit, Nanette. That's why I didn't say anything."

No, I was long past holding back my feelings. I was absolutely freaking out at this news. I zipped up the hoodie I'd just put on, even though it was still warm from the greenhouse lamps above. I took a step back. "What do you mean? Are there more of them? Are they coming after us—"

He waltzed over and wrapped his arms around me but didn't squeeze very hard. I'm sure he thought I was too physically fragile still. And perhaps I was.

"It's all right," he said and then immediately let go, as if he'd forgotten himself. His colder, more distant self kicked in.

"It's not all right," I spat. I was moving toward hysterics. But I couldn't help it. I barely survived my last encounter with Buster's men and my ex. I knew I couldn't survive another.

"First," Joey jumped in, speaking directly to me, "we don't know these men are even associated with the trucks we saw." His West Texas drawl was controlled, not as thick as normal. Second, the trucks we saw could have been military."

"Third," Ron added, "I'm going to check them out today, and confirm their identity and whether or not they might be a threat to us."

"What?" Joey snapped. "Why would you even consider this, Ronald?"

They had obviously both forgotten about my sensibilities at this point.

Ron huffed out a long breath. "I am tired of always being surprised and then reacting, rather than being proactive. So I figured If I went out before sunset, I could approach from the north of Buster's compound—the same way you and I entered—but this time, I would just verify what was going on. If we had a problem, I would let you know. At least we would be more ready for it. And after these two," he pointed at the body, "I know we'd have to be better prepared than we have been."

"I'm not disagreeing with your logic, but you're not going alone," Joey stated with a drawl more akin to those from the Southwest part of Texas.

"Thanks, but I'd rather you stayed here with Dog and looked after the women."

That was it! I hated when men said things like this; it reminded me of Bud. And I was not a big fan of Bud or his ilk at this point. For some reason—probably because my emotions sought a simpler release—I was reminded of 1979 when Billy Jean King took on the chauvinistic Bobby Riggs. My match of the sexes was against two chauvinistic men. I smashed my forehand right at their faces. "Because us little women couldn't possibly take care of ourselves." I tossed my head back and feigned light-headedness. Theatrics often helped in tennis matches.

Ron glared upward, like a hurt pup. "I didn't mean it that way, Nanette. But the last two times I left you... Well, we know what happened."

He was trying to save face, but he did have a point. So I lobbed the next shot. "I agree with Joey on this. I don't like the thought of you going out alone."

"What she said," Joey volleyed back on my behalf, quite unexpectedly. "Your whole reasoning for going now makes sense, but it doesn't make sense for you to go alone. If you are stopped at any time, then you can't warn us. You need another set of eyes, and I can back you up. Dog will be here to protect them." Joey threw a demure glance at me. "Not that you or Chloe can't protect yourselves."

Game. Set. Match.

Finally, Ron nodded at his defeat.

"All right," Ron said. "Let's get this body out into the cold with the other one. Then maybe Nanette and I can button up the place. The temperature in here is dropping way too much for our plants."

"Let me first go update Chloe and Leticia. I'll be right back," Joey said and then shuffled for the door.

Ron watched Joey leave, and then gazed back at me. "I promise we'll be careful. We're only going to find out what the military trucks are doing at Buster's place, and then we're coming back. And if we hear anything, we'll call to warn you. But just in case there are more, secure all the shutters and then you four need to get to the basement hiding place." His lips opened, about to say something more... something else heavy, like one of his many secrets. But then his gaze shot to the ground, his lips closed, and he looked up again. "Just stay here and wait for us, okay?"

I hesitated, wanting to ask what he was about to say, but didn't. Instead, I just nodded. "Yes!" Of course, my gut was saying, 'Hell no!' about all of this. Then thinking about Chloe and Leticia, I felt a sense of urgency for their mission.

"What are you doing?" Ron asked, as I slipped one arm through my winter coat.

"I'm going to help you drag the body out, so you can get going."

He looked at me with his caring eyes once again. I really appreciated this Ronald Ash.

"Are you sure you're up to it?" He must have known he couldn't talk me out of it, but he had to do the manly thing and try.

"Yep, but let's get to it before I change my mind."

We pulled the body out through the new opening. I let Ron grab the bloody arm. We then dragged each of the two bodies all the way to the next property. I was sweating profusely by the time we were done, even though it must have been close to zero outside. Plus, my body still ached everywhere. I'm pretty sure it was never going to stop aching.

The whole time, neither of us said a word. I think Ron was also a little in shock from this event. At least I hoped he was.

I worried that killing a man was something that got easier each time you did it. I only did it once and that was enough for me. But I feared what was required of Ron to survive, while at the same time do things to keep us safe, was going to change him into something I didn't care to think about.

Most of our actions were a blur. We sealed up each piece of plastic with clear packing tape, me from the inside, and Ron from the outside.

By the time we both met in the living room, Joey had already put together the equipment they needed. And just like that, Ron and Joey left us alone to deal with our own ghosts.

Dog, who must have a sixth sense or something, barked as if to say, "At least I didn't leave you alone."

Only a few minutes later, he would bark again.

CHAPTER 3

Silas "Trout" Guzman - Recording #50:11:16 - 16:05

I almost had a heart attack when I saw OP jam his pig-sticker hard into his victim's soft skin. OP grunted loudly after achieving his justice. He licked his chops, his eyes wild. Then he yanked the knife out and did it again.

I shuddered at this display. Anyone else would have probably pissed their pants.

He just sat there, near his dead son's bloodstains, imagining that he was knifing a hole into his son's killer. Instead, the receiving end of his revenge was the desk. He fisted his switch blade and stabbed the same spot, close to the corner of the desk. He sighed and then yanked it out. He did this again, and again, and again.

Most men passed the time imagining their last prostituta or compañera... Ahh, sorry, Chilo. But my boss spent every second of every day preparing for the revenge of his son.

He had used this same knife to take down many enemies in the past, including his own boss, to rise to the top of the cartel he now ran. He was determined to use it again. And because I knew he would kill me if I didn't find his son's killer, his knife was the only thing on my mind too.

So I stood there in his doorway, staring at this man who looked like El Diablo—you know, the devil—not daring to say a word while he continued to stab at the desk. I knew from experience not to speak to OP until he gave me permission to speak.

It was one of his absolute rules and we all knew this well. We also knew that not following this rule meant you'd find out what it was like to be the desk. I have seen it happen many times before.

Finally, OP must have sensed me, like a wild animal senses its prey, because he looked up and beckoned me closer. "What do you have for me, Trout?"

"Team One has not reported in, OP." I said this as I marched over toward him. "And your brilliant plan appears to have worked." It is always smart to blow smoke up the ass of the mass-murderer who is waving around the knife that had been used in many killings.

I stopped before him, partially unfolding a map I had brought to show him. He stood up from the desk, still fisting his knife as if he were getting ready to use it again.

But I didn't hesitate. I laid out the map over the table and explained what I meant. "Teams Two through Six have all reported in"—my forefinger stabbed at different points on the map to highlight each location—"but Team One has not, and they are over an hour late since their last broadcast." I double-tapped Team One's intended location on the map.

We'd agreed that each of the six two-man teams had a different area to investigate, as identified by Buster's own map. Each team was composed of expendable men, tasked with checking out their assigned locations. They would knock down doors, kill any threats, and try to take at least one, but preferably two prisoners, who would be tortured into telling us what they knew about Buster's death. OP's thinking was that we would either get a lead into Buster's death, or if a team didn't report in, then it told us we had identified the prime location of Buster's killer. We would then redirect all of our teams to that primary location, with orders to kill everyone except two survivors, who would be brought back for interrogations.

Even if the people at that location weren't directly responsible for his son's death, OP would gain some satisfaction in knowing he'd done something to avenge his son's murder.

"We've tried to contact Team One once every ten minutes, but we have heard nothing back from them."

I glanced up from the map just as OP's arm came down in a quick arc. I caught just a slight glint of the knife blade, not even able to react to it because it was coming so fast.

His pig-sticker plunged deep into the map, dead center in the circle around Team One's area, probably drawn by Buster himself.

OP had a gleam in his eye, perhaps the first I had seen since the tsunami had wiped out his home on the coast, killing his wife and all his other children.

"Send everyone to Team One's location. Kill them. Kill them all!"

CHAPTER 4

Nan

Our view of the world was reduced to what we could see out of our five-inch shutter holes, though Chloe had it much easier than me.

When Chloe and I had decided to stand watch for more bad guys, I volunteered to take the front door; she would watch the door leading out the back of the garage. Leticia asked that Dog come with her to the basement.

Front door watch, as I had thought, proved to be more difficult, even with the skinny barstool I had dragged out to make it a little more comfortable for me to wait out my period on watch. However, each time I wanted to "scan my perimeter," as Joey had described it, I had to stand up to see.

The micro-thin slits in the rolling steel shutters, which protected each of the home's windows and doors, were nearly impossible to see through. So Ron had cut five-inch holes, using his welder, through the front door shutter and the garage's back-door shutter. The front-door hole was positioned at standing eye-level, so we could see through the front door's peephole. But that provided only enough perspective to see just a few feet beyond the hole. The only way to see all around the front was to get up close to it, and that meant being on the other side of the wood door. But when I sat on the bar stool, I'd have to pop up out of my seat to see anyone or anything coming our way from the street. Chloe had it much easier indeed.

The hole cut in the shutter outside the garage's back door was at chest-level. Not sure why Ron did that, but because of this, from where Chloe sat, she didn't have to get up the whole time. Plus, it was much warmer in the garage, even with its wood door open, than in my little area outside the front door. I was freezing on my watch.

It was during these quiet times that I'd stop and consider the irony of my life and my being so good to the woman who essentially stole my ex-husband from me—regardless of how miserable my ex turned out to be. But then I considered if it weren't for my husband's infidelity with Chloe, I wouldn't have found Ron and my life would have surely ended as quickly as it did for many in our town from the flood. Really, it was only because of Chloe that I learned who my husband really was. So it was easy to forgive her for being stupid enough to have carried on with him. God knows I was stupid enough to have married the bastard.

However, this line of thinking always led me to that dark place when I had to kill him. Plastered in my mind's eye was that indelible image of his dead face, mouth permanently fixed open, gasping for the air that I had robbed him of.

An earth-rattling shudder rippled through me.

I did my best to shake away the mental effigy, but my shivers continued.

It was so damned cold today. My winter clothing and the wind-protected area, between the closed wooden door and the rolling shutter, did nothing to shut out the biting temperatures. My blood felt like it began to freeze each time I'd sit.

So I stood up for the umpteenth time, more to wrestle back control of my body warmth than anything else, and peered through the hole. I expected nothing, as always. Still, I followed the routine Joey taught me.

Look first to my left, catching just the far front edge of Ron's house, and then scan from left to right, in little square, fifty-foot grids, until I slowly ended up at the empty space on my right that once contained Sarah and Bob's neighbor's house, which had since been destroyed by the last earthquake. The only visible evidence of the neighbors even having a house was the most forward corner of what remained of their wood picket fencing. Both sides of the fence slats abruptly ended where a ragged cliff now began.

Something moved.

I was just about to sit down, after seeing nothing more than branches shake within the white scene of nothingness outside, when I caught a flash out of my left periphery.

I drilled my glare to a point where I thought I saw movement, thinking it was just one more piece of debris in the multitude of dead debris being tossed around by our perpetually blowing Arctic winds.

There it is.

My shudder returned when I saw him.

At the mouth of the cul-de-sac was a man dressed in a white camo outfit, obviously designed to blend in with the snow. If it weren't for his dark skin, long black beard, and crazy hair, I might not have seen him at all. Strapped to his back was a rifle not unlike the rifles that Ron and Joey each carried. This wasn't some scraggly survivor, looking for food like the two we killed. This was a man on a specific mission, with the resources to carry it out.

The man's head appeared to be pointed in my direction.

More unnerving, he was looking directly at me through binoculars.

I sat back hard, my heart rattled in my chest, and my shivers took on full control.

The man had to have seen me, as I could see him clearly without the aid of binoculars like he had.

I ventured another glance—I had to know what this man was planning and if there were others.

He's gone.

There was no sign of him—my eyes darted around my viewing hole. There was no sign of anyone.

Shit-shit-shit.

I made a ton of noise fumbling with the front door handle, clunking my stool and my gun against it. Once it was opened, I bolted for inside, tripping on and knocking over the stool I'd been sitting on. I left it toppled over inside the open doorway and ran.

I had to get to the garage and find out if Chloe also saw someone. I assumed Camo Man must have seen me and then, knowing his cover had been blown, he went into hiding. If it was just him watching us, that would have been one thing; it would have been creepy, but maybe not a world-ender. However, I felt fairly certain he wasn't alone. That brought more shudders as I thought that maybe he or they would try what the other two earlier intruders attempted, while we were most vulnerable. Why does this always happen when Ron is gone?

The distance between the front door and the garage entrance was maybe forty steps, but it felt like a mile as my cold legs, which had spent a month atrophying, were still not acting like they should. Meanwhile, I was breathing so hard, I thought I might pass out.

Finally, I banged against the kitchen-side interior entrance of the garage.

Once opened, I halted in the doorway and gulped back my thundering breaths.

Chloe was standing, rigid, wide-eyed, mouth agape like she was ready to shriek. Her eyes were fixed on the small hole cut in the shutter as if it were the eye of a monster staring back at here. Or perhaps a monster was on the other side.

I pulled back the hammer of my revolver, sure I'd have to put a bullet in some sonofabitch about to come through the door—if I could just control my breathing, which made my shudder that much worse.

A few shuffle-steps toward her put me into full view of the exterior doorway, and I let out a breath. I glared at the closed shutter, attempting to pick up any movement outside that the little hole offered.

I sensed nothing.

"What did ya see?" I whispered. "Was it a guy in camo?"

She just stood there like a statue, unwilling or perhaps unable to say anything. Only her blond hair fluttered from the wisps of wind that had worked their way through the circular opening in the shutter.

"What?" I insisted, a little too loudly, because whomever she saw outside would have certainly heard me.

Finally, she pointed, her face still locked into a strange scream-like trance, similar to the anxiety-ridden character in The Scream, the famous Evard Munch painting.

I marched over to her doorway, my gun still extended out in front of me. The wood door was wide open, with the shutter providing the only barrier between the outside threat she'd seen and us inside.

Bending over, I glanced through the opening—exactly the same as mine, only much lower.

My gun barrel, right below my face, tracked onto each object my eyes darted to.

Nothing outside moved. Only tree branches and—

Something.

A blur of brown and white, just beyond the tree line. It was so quick all I caught was a glance.

"A wolf?" I whispered.

Turning back to Chloe, I thought I understood immediately. She was deathly afraid of wolves—some incident in her past that I couldn't remember. Only that she was terrified by them. And after hearing some howling outside a few times and seeing paw prints, she wouldn't step foot outside because of them. I understood fear as well as anyone, and I knew how debilitating fear could be. But we didn't have time for this. A real threat loomed outside. Not some imagined one by a scavenger like a wolf.

I clicked the wood door closed, cutting off the outside wind-sounds. Finally, I flicked the deadbolt into its locked position, even though it probably didn't matter. It was more for our own psyches.

At least Chloe's mouth shut.

"Okay Chloe," I practically hollered. "I closed and locked the door." There was no need for whispering now. "The wolf can't get in." I grabbed her shoulders and put my face up to hers. "Chloe, this is important. You're safe from the wolf."

"It-it..." she gulped back her words. "It wasn't a wolf."

I wasn't sure if I should slap her or punch her at this point. She wasn't acting lucid.

"Chloe, what was it if not a wolf?"

"A-a man. He walked by the door. Like-like he knew I was there, and said, 'You're mine.' And then he was gone."

CHAPTER 5

Ron

"Hard to believe this is still Texas, ain't it?" Joey said in a mimicked down-home drawl.

His attempt at humor couldn't quite break our disquiet.

His words, though, couldn't have been more correct.

The outside was something more akin to a Vermont winter-scape, with everywhere as far as our eyes could see—which wasn't that far—smothered in a gray-white.

It was hard to believe how much our world had changed in the forty-four days since the wall of water wiped out my town: The stinky ash fell, the temperatures dropped, and then the snow started falling. Must have been a couple feet of the stuff on the ground by now.

"At least the smell is mostly gone," I said.

"Amen, brother. I couldn't get used to what smelled like a thousand broken eggs, rotting in the sun," he replied, with less of a drawl.

"Also, I'm glad we can no longer see the bodies." I said this more to myself and then turned my gaze back to the road in front of us. We had just passed the humps of several of the dead on the side of our road, They had been left there, discarded like bags of trash ahead of a trash day that would never arrive. Anyone still left, including us, just ignored the dead. There were too many of them.

But now they were being covered up. The world was doing its usual task of carpeting over its refuse, just as it has done for a thousand generations before us, leaving the bones of the past for future archaeologists to find and decipher. I wondered what their theories would say about us in a few hundred years.

"Stop!" Joey hollered.

It was like my own brain had issued the command, as I'd instantly reacted, jamming on the brakes before the "p" in "stop" had leapt out of Joey's mouth.

We slid to a stop, the rear of the Range Rover fishtailing slightly into the oncoming empty lane.

"What?" I whispered, my eyes darting everywhere, looking for whatever threat he'd seen. It was hard to see anything in the near darkness of a cloud-filled twilight, especially without turning on our headlamps.

"There." He pointed to the other side of our empty residential road.

I didn't see it at first, because it had faded some from the wind's eroding effects, the continual snowfall, and so little ambient light.

"Tire tracks," he stated, in case I hadn't seen the wide tracks, on the other side, which ran the length of the road as far as I could see ahead of us.

I still didn't acknowledge him, as I was just trying to calculate how old these tracks were. Twisting back in my seat, I could see our own prominent tracks trailing off into the darkness. Beside them, I could barely make out the other tracks, made more stark by the red glare of my brake lights.

"They're less than a day old," I mumbled, still considering the implications. The last time we'd driven down that side of the road was days ago. Someone in a vehicle with a much wider wheelbase than our Rover had driven toward our neighborhood within the last 24 hours, maybe within the past hour. Since we didn't notice it until now, there was no way to know if the vehicle—a Hummer came into my mind—passed through without going back and checking out our neighborhood to investigate further. Perhaps it was from the two men we'd just killed. If we had the time, we would have checked it out. But we couldn't risk it: Both of us felt the countdown to an inevitable fate. We knew we needed to be proactive about what we both suspected was coming our way.

"We have to get to Buster's compound quick and verify they're no longer a threat," I stated resolutely, and threw the truck into gear.

"What about the girls?" Joey asked, his gaze still fixed behind us.

"They'll be safe. And they'll call us if there's a problem." I tapped my earpiece, connected to my radio to demonstrate and verify that he understood.

He nodded as the Rover's wheels spun in the snow until I eased off the accelerator. We moved forward and built up our speed as fast as I dared.

There were more tracks, more prominently carved in the snow, the closer we got.

On the long straightaway, I picked up our speed past the point of safety.

Joey, to his credit, said nothing.

We parked in the same place that we had when we stormed Buster's compound what seemed like years ago. It was only a few weeks.

Each of us snapped and zippered up our winter gear tight before stepping out into the cold. Joey cinched his black knit hat down around his ears. I wore my Cubs cap and a wool scarf as my only head and ear protection. It would be warm enough. Although, looking in the rear-view mirror, I questioned my thinking about wearing a bright blue ball cap, which would stand out against the white landscape, and make my head an easy target.

But it's low light and at least it's not something as stark as diamondback-red, I reasoned with myself.

We agreed to split up. Joey would go toward the front of the compound; I'd take the back. We would stay out of sight and not engage anyone we saw, unless we absolutely had to. Because of the potentiality of a large force, neither of us wanted to risk taking them on by ourselves.

After a radio check, confirming that we could hear each other through our earpieces, we turned in opposite directions and plotted our different ways to our target.

A quick glance back confirmed Joey trudging away from me. Only then did I notice that he was limping. He didn't say a thing. No complaints, not even a grunt. He must have still had been in pain after the injuries he'd sustained earlier. That kid was as tough as a bear and built like one too. A very small but lethal bear.

I pushed forward, attempting to move slow enough to hear any others who might be around, but not to be heard. Not just because we agreed to it, the last thing I wanted was to have to be put in the position to have to shoot any anyone again. But deep down I knew this was probably a false hope. And with that thought, my anxiety spiked again.

But there was something else that was needling up my anxiety. I didn't know if it was something I had missed, something I didn't do but should have done.

What the hell was it?

Then it hit me.

With each step I took, moving myself farther around this vacant area, toward the river and the back of the compound, a feeling grew stronger that someone was watching my every move.

CHAPTER 6

Compton

I couldn't believe what crept in front of the crosshairs of my ocular: a bright blue Cubs baseball hat.

I almost fell out of my blind.

My sole job was to keep an eye on this compound, watching who was coming and going from my vantage point, all the while I was hidden in the neck of a giant bald Cypress. After completing my surveillance, my plan was to radio The Patriots. This was the group I hung with then. I had known it would be a long and cold wait up there. But what the hell else was I doing then?

The Patriots were just my meal ticket, until I figured a way to continue on to Mexico. They weren't military, former or otherwise. Worse, they were military wannabes: all of them laymen with guns, and no training on how to use them. Most of them had waited —some had been wishing—for the end of the world to happen. They got their wish. Well, sort of. You see, many of them truly believed the end would come as a zombie apocalypse or that there would be some sort of biological madness turning humans into violent murderers. Regardless, they were sure they would be fighting either crazy or dead humans, which they could whack at like in some video game. So in preparation, they had stockpiled ice picks, axes, scythes and other useless weapons. And when the apocalypse turned out to be a series of natural catastrophic events, followed by a new ice age, most of these men and a few women were ill equipped to deal with it. Who was?

Not only had they not stored their supplies properly, but they also didn't count on earthquakes destroying most everything they had stored. But it was the frigid temperature drop that froze whatever resolve they had left.

I would have preferred to have hooked up with some Three Percenters instead. They were who I was looking for. But you can't choose who you'll run into in an apocalypse.

Thinking back to their ridiculous initiation ceremony caused me automatically to scratch at the rough-hewn Roman numeral three tattoo scraped into my cheek. My requirement for admittance had long since healed, but it itched in the cold.

When I ran into this group, a couple of weeks ago they were desperate. They'd long since raided most of the homes and businesses around them. When that wasn't enough, they had started their expanded consumption of supplies from homes and businesses south of them.

Then they found this place. They said it had boat loads of supplies. Of course, they also said they had killed the previous owners to get access. But I didn't believe it for a minute. There is no way The Patriots, a motley group of idiots if there ever was one, could have raided this compound of well-armed men, even if there were only a skeleton crew around at the time, and caught 'em off guard.

Per my previous intel—which was obviously old—when I had passed through town before running into The Patriots, this place was controlled by a disorganized drug cartel. They seemed addled by their own drug use and so the place was ripe for the picking if someone had the balls and enough men to do it. Being one man, I had moved on. But now, these people did not look disorganized.

My guess was that The Patriots had stumbled across the drug-addled group who had previously occupied this place. They either killed that group by sheer dumb luck or more likely, someone had done it for them. Then The Patriots had started to clean out the place when the cartel's friends or the rest of their clan returned. And this group was more serious than the group that had occupied the place before them.

The Patriots wanted to return to the compound, kill everyone and clean out the rest of the supplies. I suggested they wait and learn before moving forward. "Intelligence gathering is everything," I told them. And good thing I had them hold up, because they would have had better luck surviving a leap off a mountain than raiding these people.

I offered them a better plan. Let me do what I was good at: assessing and figuring out this group's weaknesses, with help from only a couple of their men to search the periphery of the compound.

Okay, I admit it, I was really going to use those two men as bait. One or two of the bumbling fools would surely stumble and get caught by this group and probably killed. But I would be able to see firsthand how this target group would react to an outside threat. This would tell me their weak points so that we could really assess how to take the compound. Assuming that was even possible.

Of course, I didn't tell them this part, only that I would be monitoring the compound from a vantage point, without ever being seen. Then after my assessment, I could tell them if it was possible to take down the compound, so they could take all of the compound's supplies. Like I said, they were pretty desperate.

At first they didn't want to accept my plan: They thought of themselves as so badass that they'd march in with guns blazing; their own version of Shock and Awe. But in the end, I appealed to their sense of survival, and they accepted my suggestions without much more debate. I'd already proven my mettle to them before.

As a Navy SEAL, this was what I was trained to do. Being stealthy was easy. So I snuck in close and watched the compound from my high vantage point to judge its strengths and weaknesses. In less than an hour, I knew enough, without sacrificing any of The Patriots. This place was going to be too tough to invade. There were just too many well-armed and well-trained soldiers here. There had to be easier pickings somewhere else.

I had determined I would slither down the tree, get back to the main road and call in, before any of The Patriots showed up. No sense in any of them dying uselessly. But I couldn't do this until Cubs Hat was far enough away that I wouldn't be seen. And he was taking too damned long.

Isn't it time for a patrol? my brain begged.

Roughly once every half hour, one of two sentries would patrol outside the fence line.

I pulled away from my eyepiece and glanced at my watch; it was time.

A quick scan and I picked up Shorty. As I had thought, it was the shortest of the two men who patrolled the outside fence line. He may have been height-challenged, but this man was thick and formidable looking. I'd have to stay in my blind for a bit longer.

I glanced back at Cubs Hat, who had suddenly turned and was now slowly making his way to the only break in the property's fence line. This man was interesting to me.

He was obviously a civvy. But I gave him kudos for attempting to be careful in watching his six. He had already surprised me, so he was quiet enough. But he was also careless: He looked like he was walking right into the compound, without first doing his recon. If he had done this, he would avoid the trap he most obviously was about to walk into.

Since I was stuck here, I figured I'd watch the show. Like I said, what the hell else was I going to do?

Besides, with Cubs Hat's actions, I had the opportunity I was looking for. In fact, it was more than I have could asked for: Cubs Hat and Shorty were on a collision course. Now, I could see how the patrol reacted and confirm my suspicions about the place: whether or not these guys were as formidable as they seemed. And with a little luck, perhaps these two men would do some of my work for me.

I must admit, what came next was going to be fun.

My head snapped from one man to the other.

No sooner did Shorty step by me, completely unaware of my presence, when he caught sight of Cubs Hat. Shorty paused for just a second or two and then closed in on Cubs Hat from behind.

I trained my ocular on Shorty, no longer suppressing my smile.

There were times when I really enjoyed what I did. This was one of them.

Cubs Hat maintained his slow creep until he came to a halt at an opening in the fence-line, looking in every direction but behind him.

Turn around, dumbshit! I wanted to yell, almost feeling bad for what was coming his way.

Shorty approached quick and quiet, his new AK pistol —I had smelled the gun oil when he walked by the first time—pointed at Cubs Hat, finger on the trigger.

❄ ❄ ❄

Ron

My heart sank when I saw it.

Buster's compound had come into view, and I could see and hear it was alive with activity, far from being abandoned, like we left it only a few weeks ago. It was everything I was afraid of.

Our plan had been for Joey to go around to the front of the property, and I would go around to the riverside rear. Then we'd double back and meet at the break in the fence line. Whoever got there first would wait for the other.

After seeing the bustle in front of the buildings, I skipped the rear altogether. And after seeing what was going on, I wasn't sure I could wait the fifteen or so minutes we figured it would take each of us to finish our recon.

I still had no plans to engage them: It was already obvious that there were far too many of them. Now I just had to know who these people were.

From this distance, most of them looked Hispanic and that concerned me, because it supported our worry that they were part of Buster's cartel. If they were, we were no longer safe.

I had to confirm it.

A group of men seemed to be congregated by the front of what was a motel, which later became Buster's offices. That was where we had the showdown and Buster was killed.

Each of these men were dressed in white camo, military garb. Each carried at least one military-style rifle. There were a number of Humvees parked close by.

They looked like they were readying themselves for battle. But where? Here or were they going to go out and wage a war elsewhere... like on our home?

Oh, how I wished I had brought my binoculars.

I had no choice: I had to get a closer look, maybe even close enough to hear something.

The break in the fence line was only a few feet away and there was maybe a hundred-meter dash from there, through a wide-open incline, to the side of the closest building. Because everyone was facing away, it was possible no one would see me. I had to try. If I could hear them speak or see any other signs to confirm that they were cartel, I would know that was it. We'd have to leave. We'd have no choice then.

If this was cartel, they would be searching for Buster's killers. And they would eventually find us.

Images of the two men we'd just killed came to mind.

Perhaps they'd already found us and now they were getting ready to come down on us.

I slung my rifle around to my back and double-checked there was no one around.

Crack!

It was the sound of a tree limb breaking: the one just behind me, that I had stepped around to get here.

I spun around and was looking directly into the barrel of another man's rifle. He looked Mexican.

CHAPTER 7

Nan

I slammed the front door.

It's not like this would keep out whoever really wanted to come in. That's what the rolling steel shutters were for. But it was obvious someone was out there and they meant us harm.

"What exactly did this man look like?" I asked, now facing her.

Chloe's wide eyes darted past me to the door, and then back to me. "Ah... he was white—I mean dressed in white, you know, military—I mean camouflage-like uniform."

I grabbed her shoulders and drilled into her. "Go get Leticia. If she's not already down in the cellar, go there and wait for me. I'm going to call Ron and Joey and get them back here."

Chloe half-nodded, and then stared at the door again.

"Go, dammit! We need to get to the cellar, where it's safe."

Chloe took off to the bedrooms, with me behind her, but I kept going.

I pulled out the radio, spun the knob and a dull light turned on. Clicking the mic, I hollered, "Ron or Joey. There are two armed men in camo uniforms outside our home."

I opened back up the front door and stepped right up to the shutter, leaning in to see through the peep hole. I glared out and searched.

No one.

"And I don't see them anymore," I said over the radio.

Not hearing anyone, I fumbled with the volume. There was nothing. Not the tone I usually heard. Not static. And it was all the way up, on maximum volume. Still nothing.

The radio's light was out.

At that moment, I forgot which direction was on or off, and so I twisted it again until it clicked on and off and on again. Nothing.

It's dead, you idiot!

I had the thing on for so long and forgot to put it in the charging stand.

A quick glance into the kitchen's charging stand confirmed there were no other units. There was one for each of us, and Leticia must have had hers with her. So I needed to borrow hers or Chloe's.

Before heading in their direction, I checked once more out the peephole. Still no one.

I sat my radio into one of the two bases, and a red light confirmed what I had thought: I'd let the battery run down.

Chloe met me at the basement door, looking out of breath. She was about to tell me something, but I needed her radio more.

"Mine's dead and the other one is missing," I said, reaching for her unit and snapping it off her belt. She glared at me like I had slapped her.

This time a twist of the knob gave the familiar beep-tone, letting me know it was charged enough to send a signal. "Ron or Joey. We have intruders," I hollered at the radio.

Chloe grabbed my arm.

I continued with the radio. "At least two armed men in white camo uniforms are outside the house, though I don't see either right now. One made threats through the door."

Chloe was practically shaking, and desperately trying to get my attention.

I glared at her, thinking that she was just freaked out about the men, the wolves, my radio call, and life in general. But then I realized it was something else.

"What?"

The radio crackled.

"Hang on," I told Chloe. "Ron or Joey. Please report. We need you back here ASAP. We—" I let go of the mike button and glared at Chloe. "What is it?"

"She's gone," she mumbled, her eyes welling with tears, about ready to burst.

"Who's gone?" I really wasn't sure what she was talking about.

"Leticia. She's not in the house."

CHAPTER 8

Ron

"Hands up, Gringo!"

The short but thick-as-an-Oak Mexican man motioned with his short AK-47 rifle.

My hands were already up. The higher they went, the lower my heart sank.

Perhaps this isn't cartel. They're here for some other reason, I mentally yelled at myself, unconvincingly.

The man's mouth moved. But between my heart beating so hard and my earpiece squeaking, indicating someone was transmitting—the volume was too low—I missed completely what both the radio and the Mexican said.

"What?" I asked, keeping my hands thrust into the sky. I desperately wanted to put one down, so I could key in my mike and warn Nan of what I was becoming more sure of: These men knew about us.

I didn't dare try it.

Still, the man's face, carpeted with dirty gray hair, tightened into an angry scowl.

"What are you doing snooping around OP's property?" he repeated in a thick accent.

The radio continued, but I still couldn't make it out: "...in white ... outside the hou..." It was Nan's frantic voice, she was hollering something unsuccessfully in my ear which made no sense. I needed to get free from this man.

I hammed up a terrified and confused look on my face. I was terrified about not being able to get free, so I tried something. "I'm hungry, and I heard there was food here..." I knew this was a stupid ploy the minute the words hopped off my tongue. I had a serious rifle slung over my shoulder and a holstered handgun: I wasn't just scrounging for food. "Who is OP?" I tried.

The man snickered and then said, "Oso Polar owns this property, and this whole region. If you don't know this, you will learn it soon."

Oh shit-oh shit-oh shit!

I knew exactly who that was: Oso Polar or Polar Bear in Spanish—because he's big, white-haired and vicious as hell, like a polar bear—ran the largest drug cartel in Northern Mexico and Texas. Worse yet, I was pretty sure that it was Polar who was Buster's father, or at least a close relative... Buster had run this place, until we killed him. Perhaps they'd figured out already it was us who did it.

It was our worst nightmare.

Truck engines behind me fired up. I knew that meant the Hummers were leaving. I turned to glance back.

"Not to worry, Gringo. They're not for you. They going to go kill the people who killed OP's son and torture the survivors.

Run!

I needed to get away, even though I'd be shot. It was better than doing nothing.

"Come on, Gringo, let's see what OP wants to do with you. You're probably dead, but maybe you can tell him something he wants to hear and then you live."

"Wa-wa-will"—I could barely breathe, much less speak —"I get food?"

"Oh, you'll get something, Gringo. But I pretty sure—"

Thunk.

The heavy-set Mexican crumbled to the ground, like a giant sack of pinto beans.

Behind him was a grinning Joey.

He grabbed the Mexican's rifle, checked the chamber and slung it around his back. He felt around the big man's belt and found a radio, just like ours and then looked back at me, still grinning. But then his grin turned to a scowl.

I turned up my volume so I could hear whoever was calling on the radio and I signaled to Joey to do the same.

"Repeat. Is that you, Nan?" I begged my radio.

The Mexican groaned and writhed on the ground. He wasn't unconscious.

Then he started laughing. "You don't know what you do. OP will kill you for this. Both of you."

He wasn't scared at all, even though we were the ones holding guns on him.

Joey put his whole body into it this time and clobbered the Mexican on the back of his head. This seemed to silence, or perhaps kill the man. I didn't care at that moment.

My radio blared, "Ron or Joey. Please report. We need you back here ASAP. We—"

Joey glared his acknowledgment. He'd heard that too. Then he flicked on the Mexican's radio. There were several voices, all in Spanish.

I held the mic down on my radio and barked, "They're coming for us. Get to the basement. Go now. They are coming for you, right now... What are they saying?"

I stopped speaking, my thumb still holding the mic button down, completely focused on trying to understand what they were saying on the Mexican's radio. My Spanish wasn't fantastic, but it was good enough.

"Turn it up," I told Joey, forgetting I had the mic on my radio still open.

CHAPTER 9

Nan

"What do you mean she's gone?"

I felt like I had been sucker-punched. I just stared at Chloe, dumbfounded by her announcement.

"Where the hell could she go?" I spun on a heel, searching for some obvious sign of Leticia, as if Chloe had simply missed her.

The radio blared; Ron announced something, but I couldn't exactly hear what.

We have to find Leticia first.

I clicked the radio off. There was nothing Ron and Joey could do for us or us for them. We needed to find Leticia now.

My hand had already found the basement door handle. I gave it a twist, confirming the interior lock was engaged. This was just as we had agreed: When everyone was topside, we'd keep this door locked, unless all of us were down there.

"Are you sure you checked all the potential hiding places in every room?" I asked Chloe. I was still incredulous at her initial response, because there weren't very many spots a twelve-year old could hide in this small house.

Now it was Chloe who looked at me like I was the idiot. "Yes, of course I did," she said. "I'm telling you she definitely isn't here."

Only then did it occur to me.

"Where's Dog?"

"Oh hell. Wait..." Chloe's head snapped forward and back. "Wasn't he with you when you..."

"It's okay, they have to be together," I said in an attempt to reassure us both.

"Leticiaaa? Where are you, honey?" Chloe yelled, her voice elevating to a pitch that could have cracked glass.

I ignored her, jamming my key into the basement door lock, turning and yanking open the door. I bellowed into the basement's darkness at the top of my lungs, "Dog, here boy. Come here, Dog."

Both of us held our breaths, waiting for what we knew should follow, if he was downstairs with Leticia.

One thing I could always count on was Dog responding to our commands. He was well trained by his previous owner, and we were the benefactors of that training. If he didn't respond, that could only mean one thing.

"Oh God," Chloe breathed.

I raised my pistol into the air. At once, its weight felt monumental. Still, I held it in front of me and turned my body toward to the only place Dog and Leticia could be... hoped they could be.

My thumb found the hammer. I clicked it back hard and took a step toward the only other exit to the house we hadn't checked: the back door entry into the solarium garden.

When I opened the door, I expected to find the door's protective rolling shutter down and locked. But I also knew Leticia was able to unlock this. It was formidable for her, but she could still lift it up high enough to duck under. I couldn't imagine why she would have gone there. But it was the only other place she could have gone.

We had to open the door and check. But not just for Leticia and Dog.

If the shutter was open, this wood door could be easily penetrated by someone with a sledgehammer, like the two who were about to try and break in earlier. It was also the only way those men in white camo could easily get into the house.

"Open the door when I tell you," I whispered.

Chloe nodded, understanding exactly what I was doing. She glanced at her pistol, a black Taurus 9mm, probably for comfort, or to make sure it was ready to fire: a tiny, raised lever—painted red to indicate a live round was in the chamber—behind the slide gave her verification it was 'cocked and locked,' as my dead ex-husband liked to say all too often. Compared to mine, her weapon looked like a peashooter. But it was much more suited to her hand size than the monstrously large cannon I held, which felt like it would slip out of my sweaty mitts at any moment.

Her own gun arm lifted a little more. I corrected my aim down, about midway up the door, anticipating that's where I might have to shoot if Camo Man were there.

With her free hand, Chloe reached for the door handle, a good foot away from her. She took one last step toward it and then nodded her readiness.

Her face was skeleton-tight; her mouth lolled open in its vein attempts to capture enough air to fill her desperate lungs. I was sure I was doing the same.

"Okay," I whispered.

I aimed down my gun arm, imagining Camo Man, and where he might be standing behind the door. I was going for his head now.

In one motion, Chloe whipped open the door and my finger found the trigger.

For just a flash, I saw Bud standing there, snickering just as he did the day I killed him.

But he wasn't there. Neither was Camo Man.

Out came our breaths, as a small blast of cool air hit us.

The rolling shutter was pulled up about waist-height. But no one was there.

It was quiet other than a dull hum of someone speaking, in the distance.

I held up a palm to keep Chloe in her place and ducked underneath the shutter to do a quick scan of the greenhouse.

The light was not on, and so the only illumination was from what was creeping out from house under the shutter, along with the soft glow of the space heater we had on to keep the room warm enough so that the plants wouldn't die.

"Do you see them?" Chloe breathed from behind me.

I flicked on my mini-Maglite and scanned the entire space.

"No..." I said. My glare hung at the place in the plastic where the intruder had come in. Ron had duct-taped it to temporarily seal out the cold. He and Joey were planning on throwing on some panels later today, after they had confirmed it was safe.

A long piece of the packing tape hung down, exposing the cut opening in the plastic. It had definitely been pushed aside, meaning someone had gone through the opening. Someone was here. Someone had come in.

I retreated back under the shutter, banging my back in the process. I gave the shutter a stiff yank, bringing it down with a crash. I hesitated over the lock; my stomach turned somersaults.

"What are you doing?" Chloe squawked like a surprised bird.

All I had to do was snap the lock and its heavy deadbolt would slide into the concrete, making our house virtually impenetrable. "I know Ron and Joey told us to lock up the house the moment we saw anyone outside." I let go of the lock.

"So you're not going to lock the shutter?" Her pitch was even higher.

I shook my head. "If Leticia and Dog are outside, they wouldn't be able to get back in. And Ron and Joey are locked out too."

Chloe nodded. "But what about the men we saw; won't they be able to get in easy?"

I slammed the wood door and locked it and turned to Chloe. "We're going downstairs and waiting, with our weapons. If the Camo Men break in, we'll hear them make noise and we'll have to get ready to defend ourselves. If Leticia returns, hopefully she has her key to the basement door... or she'll knock and announce herself... The guys can take care of themselves."

Once again returning my focus to the radio, I pointed to the basement door, so that Chloe would unlock it, and I twisted the volume control.

"... to the basement. They're coming for us. Get to the basement..."

Chloe's and my eyes locked into each other, as she flung open the door.

"... What are they saying?" Ron asked someone in the distance.

Chloe darted into the basement's darkness, and then slapped the wall where the wall switch was. Light glared from below.

"Turn it up," Ron instructed but not to us. His voice echoed below, as I closed and locked the door behind me and took the steps down two at a time.

"... Nos acercamos a la casa," a staticky voice said in Spanish in the background of my radio. And that Spanish voice reverberated downstairs, as if from another radio. I spoke Spanish, so I knew what was being said. We are approaching the house.

We both practically tumbled all the way down the stairs, Chloe leading, then rushing out of sight.

At the base of the stairs, I saw Chloe slumped over the small table we often shared. On it sat one of our radios—Leticia's handheld radio—and beside it was her much larger ham radio with coiled microphone beside it. In between the radios was Leticia's bright yellow voice recorder. The little red light was on the recorder, indicating it was recording now.

Leticia never went anywhere without her recorder, which meant she left in a hurry.

The Spanish on Leticia's and my handheld continued.

CHAPTER 10

Leticia Brown - Audio Recording #32

When I heard that voice, it sent shivers down my spine.

I had been sitting in my spot, with Dog keeping me company—he's great company—while I worked to find other people on the ancient portable ham radio Ron had dug up in Sarah's attic for me. That's when I came across the signal.

Unfortunately, the portable antenna didn't pick up much down here. Ron said he was going to set me up a 40-meter dipole antenna outside—I even gave him the wire measurements—but he also said he had been busy with all of his projects, that he would get to it the next day. It was always the next day with him. But I wasn't angry with him.

Earlier today, because I couldn't wait any longer, I strung out a little wire antenna in the basement and promised myself I would try each day to find other ham broadcasts. I couldn't broadcast back, if I even wanted to. With my little antenna and the unit's low wattage, it wouldn't transmit far enough, if even out of the basement. But I could listen.

So today I tried to find some transmissions. And after about an hour of striking out looking for ducks, I found my first quack.

You see, on single side-band radio, when voices are transmitting on a frequency near yours, they sound like ducks speaking. All you have to do is just tune into them until their voices are clear.

So when I heard the broadcast, I began the process of slowly tuning into it. Then it was gone. And now I couldn't find any sign of it.

"Where are you, ducks!" I yelled at the stupid thing.

I adjusted the squelch some more and then continued to inch back the channel selector, attempting to be as gentle as possible, not wanting to miss the channel when either Donald or Daffy began speaking again.

Oh, I should probably explain why I'm recording this.

Um... Besides, being a ham operator and lover of science—my parents used to call me their little genius, which I'm not sure was true—I am a budding writer. I like to write stories, because they are often so much more interesting than real life.

But most great story ideas actually come from real life. So I like to record some of the real life anecdotes I have experienced or heard about, to remind me of some of my future storylines.

But it's also because sometimes I have things to tell my new friends, and it's just easier to record what I'm thinking and let them play it back rather than telling them directly.

I guess I still feel uncomfortable speaking to people most of the time, even my friends. Ever since... That evil man killed my parents.

Anyway, I thought it would be good to talk to my recorder—another Ronald gift—and describe what I'm doing, so I didn't have to do it in person. And what I don't like, I can delete and start again. So, that's why I'm doing—

"CQ-CQ-C..."

My tuning hand held up again and I glared at the radio, almost too afraid to touch the channel selector. But I knew what to do.

I clicked it forward a couple of millicycles when it belted out the call again. This time it was Donald, and before I lost it, I tuned directly into the correct frequency until he came in loud and clear.

"CQ-CQ-CQ. This is Black... for anyone who is interested in sanctuary from the cold. We have a protected sanct... plenty of food and... we may need you. If you have..." The radio signal bled away to nothing.

"No, don't go," I yelled at the radio.

The signal was gone.

What sucks was that it could have been close by, or it could have been on the other side of the world. Unless he calls again, I will never know.

I pulled out the logbook, and made a note of the frequency, the time and what was said.

Grrrrr.

I gave Dog a look. He was on the floor, but sprang up, his head pointed upward and alert.

Another voice.

It was coming from the handheld.

I could also hear the muffled voice of Chloe yelling something upstairs.

I turn up the handheld.

"Nos acercamos a la casa," one voice said.

"Ya estamos en la retaguardia," answered another.

"It's nothing but Spanish, Dog," I whispered, even though no one could hear me above the racket from the radio. I know it's bad, though.

"C'mon, Dog. Follow me."

Audio Transcript Begins

[Noises of a chair being slid across a concrete surface, followed by footsteps.]

"Two here. There's no one in back," said another voice.

"Three here. There's no one on either side of the house," still another voice said.

[More noises of scraping and slamming shut of a door.]

"One here. We made visual contact with at least one female earlier. So we know they are in the house. Do I have your permission to enter the house, OP?"

"Do it now!" demanded someone in a deep voice.

Boom!

Bang-bang-bang!

Audio Transcript Ended

CHAPTER 11

Ron

We raced back without saying a word to each other.

The radio we had jacked from the Mexican was on full volume, wedged between the dash and the windshield. And we listened to it the whole way. During a nerve-wracking period of silence in the broadcasts, Joey tried to call out to Nan and Chloe on our radio.

There was no answer.

We each knew enough Spanish to get what was happening. OP's men had stormed the house. And based on the short bursts of gunfire, it sounded like a one-way battle.

During the last broadcast, OP's troops announced they had killed all but one survivor, a pretty young woman who they were bringing back to their compound to torture.

Nothing more was said.

"Nan? Chloe? Leticia?" Joey cried out, his voice broken and raw.

I was a different kind of raw.

As we pulled into our street, my building anger turned into a blinding rage that hit me like a freight train, threatening to run over anything and anyone in its path.

"Have they left?" Joey asked. I wondered this too. We couldn't do anything about our loved ones, but we could do something about these murderers.

I glared at him.

He was checking his weapon, making sure it was ready, and preparing to bolt out of the Rover.

The house was completely black.

We slid to a stop in front of the house, and both of us hopped out into the snow.

Joey dashed out in front, almost as nimble as he was when I first met him. I pulled up the rear. We both raced.

Everything seemed off, not at all what I expected.

And then I realized why. A thousand little puzzle pieces locked together, and a picture formed.

"The shutter is locked," Joey said, yanking at the front door shutter. Then he trained his flashlight on the ground and moved the beam along the garage-side of the house.

"And did you notice that we didn't pass any vehicles?" I huffed, verbalizing my thoughts.

"I mostly only see our footprints here..."

He was right. At best, I only saw one set that wasn't ours. But not the expected mob of boot prints from OP's army of men.

"Out back," Joey whispered and scurried around the path, to the garage. I followed his lead, clicked on a flashlight, and dashed around the other side, just in case we were wrong.

The now-expected oddities continued: There was only one set of human footprints, though even they seemed kind of faded. And several recent paw prints by a wolf.

My mind replayed the scene we'd just verbally witnessed at OP's compound before we'd left.

At least two Humvees took off with maybe eight to ten men. And the radio broadcast made it sound like there were at least that many at the sight of incursion. There should have been more signs of their being there.

Unless they had approached from a different street, and had gone through the back...

I gulped back this realization and pumped my legs through the heavy snow as fast as I could make them go, until I saw Joey push through the many-times-breached plastic covering of the greenhouse.

I was just a few seconds behind him.

Joey was already all the way through the greenhouse and was pushing open the wood entrance to the house when I poked my head through the sliced opening and saw the shutter was rolled all the way up. Joey's light disappeared from the doorway.

I cast my light around the inside of the greenhouse, while pushing through the two-by-fours that framed the breached opening, and then beelined it to the door, not caring at that point what patch of growth my feet trampled.

"Chloe?" Joey yelled, out of sight.

I fumbled with my rifle as I reached the open doorway.

Low rumbles sounded behind me.

I halted at the doorway and turned back toward the opening in the plastic we'd just come through and listened for everything. Anything.

"Nan, Leticia, Dog, are you there?" Joey yelled, more distant.

Muffled sounds of a dog barking, women's voices, and something else.

It sounded like thunder in the distance.

"We're here!" hollered Nan deep from within the basement.

I let go of a gasp I'd been restraining.

The rumbles continued.

The final piece of this puzzle clicked into place. I knew exactly what the rumbles were. I took a long breath and stepped through the doorway.

Joey had the basement door open, its light pouring out.

A thunder of footsteps up the stairs.

"Oh my God," Joey said. "I thought they had gotten you."

Chloe leapt out of the basement doorway in a single bound, and into Joey's awaiting arms.

Nan followed and wrapped her arms around me.

Dog barreled into me, nearly sending both of us to the ground, and promptly licked my hand with his slobber-laden tongue.

Even Leticia wrapped her arms around Joey and Chloe; the three melted together like they were one person. Her wet eyes glared at me.

"I thought we were done for when I heard the cartel coming for us, and then the booms," Nanette said breathlessly. "We turned off all the lights and the radio. And we waited for what we knew was coming for us."

"But they never came," Chloe said.

"We turned back on the radio and listened to them say they had killed us all, except one young woman," Leticia chimed in, stating this in the first long sentence I'd heard from her lips in a while. "I recorded the whole thing."

"Yeah, after you and Dog came out of hiding," Nanette chided.

"So what happened to them? If they didn't attack you, who did they attack?" Joey asked. "We definitely didn't see any sign of them here."

"I think I know why," I said. "Follow me."

Nanette held firmly to my unslobbered hand while I led them through the house to the front door.

Silently the whole group shuffled behind me through the empty house.

I opened the front door and then unlocked the shutter and rolled it upward.

"There." I pointed to the north, west of where Buster's place was.

A churning red glow flickered in the night sky. A flash and then a deeper red erupted, and a boiling cloud of smoke burrowed its way into the heavens.

"What was that?" Leticia asked.

As if in answer, a boom crackled in the distance.

"They attacked someone else, thinking it was us."

CHAPTER 12

Compton - From Recording #51B

"They were all dead, every single one of them. Even the three women were slaughtered."

Interviewer speaks softly: He scratched away at three lines on his cheek, like some festering wound that wouldn't stop bothering him.

"I'd seen some nasty stuff in war. The kind of things that humans should not be capable of doing to other humans. This was worse. Some of the Patriots were gutted. One was missing a lot of his skin and... some other parts...

"Gore never bothered me before. But maybe because I knew some of these people... Anyway, I tossed my cookies right there."

Interviewer: "What did you do next?"

"I looked for supplies. Any supplies. But they were all gone too. Taken by the same people who killed everyone. Other than the detached garage, where I believe they'd done all the torturing, the rest of the structures were burned to the ground. So I left.

"There was nothing there for me at the Patriot's base, so I bugged out..."

Interviewer: "Until you found us?"

❄ ❄ ❄

S. Guzman AKA: Trout - Audio Recording #50

"Yeah, we killed them all."

N. Thompson: "Trout, who were they?"

S. Guzman: "Who cares. Just some group of survivalists called The Patriots. But we thought they were you."

C. Evans: "Why did you think that?"

S. Guzman: "They came up on our grid search of the area, and we saw they were armed. We knew the group that hit Buster and his crew were well armed. When we searched their property, we found some of Buster's stuff and some of his supplies. Then when we tortured the one female survivor, she admitted to their theft and said their group had killed Buster. I knew it was bullshit, but OP was satisfied. So we stopped searching for you."

C. Evans: "What happened to the one you tortured?"

S. Guzman: "I gutted her on the spot... But I had to because OP was watching."

N. Thompson: "Wait. You said you stopped searching for us. But how did you find us?"

S. Guzman: Laughing hysterically.

Four Months Later

CHAPTER 13

Nan

The panel truck's back-up alarm blared so loud, I dropped the keys.

Nothing to worry about here. It's the same as before, I told myself.

Still, my hands quivered. I will never get used to that sound.

I swiped my hand across the ice-cold concrete, almost missing them, while looking back to make sure everyone was ready.

Joey stood as tall as his five-foot-one frame would allow. He leaned into the boxes of vegetables in the middle of the garage and cycled a round into the ancient-looking Winchester he held with both hands. His face looked far scarier than his rifle, whose bore was as small as a pencil lead.

Chloe was in the back of the garage, bundled up in her usual torn parka that she wore on these days. With her disheveled hair, no makeup and streaks of garden dirt across her face, she looked nearly the same age as Leticia. Her one adornment was a .38 semi-rusted, snub-nosed revolver clutched by her two shuddering hands—at least it's not just me.

Oh yeah...

A quick check of the house entrance confirmed that Leticia was not here, and neither was Dog. That was also part of their requirements: door open and "that mutt of yours is locked up when we arrive."

We were ready.

I reached out with one hand for the lock, more to steady myself than anything else, and with the other I slid in the correct key into the garage door lock and clicked it open.

I held my breath and told myself, At least we'll get Ron back today. That's what matters here. That's all that matters.

A quick yank and the garage door rolled up, revealing one Silas "El Trucha" (The Trout) Guzman. A huge grin was plastered across his disgusting mug.

"Well, good morning, Chilo," Trout said to me.

He glanced at Joey and his protruding, fish-like lips immediately pursed. "Hey-hey Chavo. We are all friends here." Trout crooked his neck and threw his arms up in exaggerated fashion, all meant to show his scorn for Joey's attempt to look threatening, backed up by his peashooter. Trout then pointed to the ground in a silent command.

Joey's gaze held, his chest lifted some, but he did as instructed and pointed his Boy Scout gun at the ground.

"You too, Chica," Trout announced to the back of the garage.

Chloe shrank in on herself, even more than usual, if that was possible. Her head lolled forward, her shoulders sank, and her little gun now hung at her side, out of view and no longer a threat. If it ever was one.

I turned back to Trout. "Where's Mr. Ash?" There was no emotion in my voice—at least I hoped there wasn't.

"Your man is just fine. OP will not damage one of his most prized assets... At least not too bad." Trout balled a fist and pounded three times on the side of the truck.

The rear panel slid up with a crash. But I couldn't see inside because of the way it was parked in our driveway.

Matador jumped out and took a swagger-filled step toward us. His long hair whipped in the wind, its greasy strands hadn't seen a shower since the apocalypse. Based on the dank odor that followed him wherever he went, perhaps he had never washed. He tossed a glance first at me and then into the garage, where he held, searching. Then his eyes finally caught a glimpse of Chloe, who failed at disappearing completely into the shadows. With this he smiled, revealing his rotted teeth. His leering glare was glued to her for way too long. Finally, he turned back to the open truck.

A hand was offered to Ron, who brushed it aside and hopped down from the tailgate, nearly slipping and falling on the icy driveway. Once his footing was sure, Ron looked up at me and forced a smile. One of his eyes was an angry shade of red and his cheek was puffy. There were at least two or three new cuts on his face, already attempting to heal over the old ones.

My stomach turned. But I tried not to gasp or show surprise. And like before, new anger filled me, adding to a growing reservoir of rage. I wanted revenge for his receiving another beating. But I didn't let it bubble up to the surface. Instead, I held it back, allowing it to simmer and ferment until sometime in the future when I knew I would have to call upon it again.

Ron signaled to Joey and croaked out, "Crane." His voice did not sound like his own.

Joey nodded, laid his rifle on the floor, and pushed the hydraulic engine hoist over to the truck.

OP was having Ron work on another engine. Bringing the engine back here was part of the agreement because Ron said the only equipment in town that he could use was either at his home or his shop, and his shop was destroyed in the flood.

It was a lie, of course. Otherwise, OP would have kept Ron at his compound and never released him. What could we do? We were beholden to this new master of our world; we had no choice... If we wanted to live.

More like survive, and just barely.

"Aren't you going to help?" Ron half-begged Matador and the driver—I didn't recognize this one—as he and Joey struggled getting the giant engine out of the truck using the lift.

"Not our job, vato," Matador said, hands on his hips. His voice was gravelly sounding, like he gargled on broken glass each morning. It was always unnerving. Trout had told us how much of a psycho-murderer this man was. So just being in his presence was unsettling, as well as destructive to our olfactory glands. "Our job is to guard you and shoot you if you don't do what we want. Entiende?"

I took a step forward.

"No, Chilo. This is not women's work," Trout insisted.

My hand tensed into a fist. With a finger through the keyring and one key protruding straight out, it would have made a lethal weapon. I pictured driving this into Trout's eye and twisting. I didn't even try to suppress a grin.

"Oh, this is funny to you, Chilo?" Trout asked. It wasn't a question. "Enough standing around. Load our things," he said, motioning to the crates of vegetables in the middle of the floor.

"I thought that wasn't woman's work," I snapped.

He leaned into me, grabbing my jaw with a gloved hand. "You have a smart mouth, Chilo. I would hate to mess up your pretty face, any more than it already is."

Out of my periphery, I saw Matador saunter to the back of the garage.

I made a quick step away from Trout's grasp, his hand hanging in the air as if he were still commanding control over my face. I turned and stepped in front of Matador, who was headed for Chloe. She shrank in the other direction and bolted forward with me between them.

"Come on," I said. "Let's get these loaded so these men can go on their way." I stated this with as much empathy as my anger would allow.

I hoisted up the top crate and lumbered past Ron and Joey, who were push-pulling the lift with a huge engine dangling from its heavy chains.

"Jose!" Trout yelled in Spanish at the lanky driver, who was about to take the box from me. "You and Matador go search the house."

"Si... But that pinche dog better not be there," Matador announced loud enough that the neighbors could hear him, if we had any. It was obviously addressed to Leticia if she was in earshot.

"The dog is in the bedroom, with Leticia. So I wouldn't suggest you open that door." This time I held back my smirk—no sense in provoking a psycho-murderer any more than was necessary.

He lifted his rifle in my direction, I'm sure hoping to get a reaction.

I ignored him and hoisted another box up, leaving the last for Chloe, who was already leaning over to pick it up. She wanted these bastards out of here as much as any of us. More.

Matador humphed, slung his rifle to his back and unholstered his pistol. When Jose caught up to him, the two men stepped through the garage entrance into the house and disappeared from sight. They would proceed to toss our house for five minutes, looking for any contraband. But mostly their actions were intended to be malicious.

They would find nothing, as they'd taken everything of value from us: our weapons, most of our food, our radios, our bug-out bags, and even our vehicle.

In the distance, Dog barked. It was muffled, but everyone understood its meaning: He would tear the men to pieces if they opened the door. I always hoped they would.

Not more than two minutes later, the two men returned. Apparently, Dog helped them to move along their search a little more quickly. It was another way Dog brought cheer to our lives.

Trout looked up and waited for their report.

Joey stood by the door, clutching his Boy Scout .22, scowling at Matador.

Matador stopped in front of Chloe and flashed his rotten grin. When he saw Trout tapping a foot impatiently, he announced, "They're clean. Except for the two weapons we gave them here."

"What, no gold-plated pistols?" Joey stated sardonically.

Trout flashed a glance at Joey and held, his eyes drilling in, as if he were making a mental note of something. But then he acted like he ignored the comment.

Joey, to his credit, held his scowl, unmoving.

Trout turned on a heel and jumped into the cab of the truck. The other men followed.

Trout didn't make his usual snarky comment about seeing each of us in two weeks. He didn't even look back.

And that's when I knew we were in trouble.

As Matador slid the truck's rear door closed, the truck engine rumbled to a start. Moments later, they slowly pulled out of the driveway, and I slid the garage door down hard.

With each new noise—the engine rumble, the tires on the ashy snow, the wheeze of the sky's diseased lungs, and finally, the deep thump of the truck door—my gut slow-tumbled over a mile-deep cliff.

Joey had just told Silas "Trout" Guzman that he knew Buster had a gold-plated gun. The only way he could have known this was if he were there. If Trout put it together and told OP, we were all screwed.

CHAPTER 14

Ron

"We cannot continue to let them come here every two weeks and take half of our food," Joey protested. His face was as red as I've ever seen.

But I was seeing red as well. "What do you want to do, mount an attack against the cartel with your .22 Boy Scout rifle, and Chloe's equally menacing snubby?" I huffed and glared past Joey. I pushed up from the kitchen table—where we always had our little post-visitation discussions—intending to walk away. There was no point in entertaining this discussion any further. None of them were serious about making the next tough decision. And I had work to do.

"I know. I know." Joey examined his feet. His shoulders slumped and his hand fell onto Chloe's shoulder, who was sitting in between Leticia and Nanette. "But dammit, we have to do something. We can't exist forever like this."

Maybe it was time to say something...

"And Nan told me while we were packing up OP's produce that we are going to run out of food at this rate," Chloe added, as she clutched Joey's hand. She glanced over at Nanette for confirmation.

Nanette flashed a look at Chloe and then at me, without saying anything. She wanted to speak on this but did not. Maybe she wasn't sure this was the place and time.

This pissed me off even more, and I decided to let all of them have it.

"We can just eat half-rations," Leticia barked, casting her watery stare at me before dropping her gaze to her feet.

I paused, with my mouth half open. It was always a shock to hear Leticia say anything more than a sigh. But that wasn't what made me pause.

Her eyes usually flashed the wisdom or sheer brilliance of someone three times her age. Now she looked every bit of a twelve-year-old, demure and hiding from something. She had suffered a lot, and probably didn't need any more to stoke her anxiety. And so it made what I needed to say seem even worse.

"More pressing now," I turned my attention back to the group, "is when they realize we had a part in Buster's killing. It may not happen today, or tomorrow. But once they connect those dots, you know they'll... come after us."

Leticia scooted her chair back from the table and dashed out of the kitchen and out of sight, no doubt into to her sanctuary in the basement. The door slam confirmed this.

I held my palm out when Nanette made like she was going to get up from the table, hunt Leticia down and speak with her. The kid needed to deal with her own guilt, just like the adults at this table needed to deal with the giant elephant in the room they had been ignoring.

"Ah, yeah. Sorry about that. It just came out. That Matador punches my buttons every time." Joey shifted on his feet, looking totally deflated. He dropped his eyes back down, as if they were too heavy to meet mine. Then they sprang back up. "But you're right about OP's men figuring us out. Maybe we should look at leaving now... You know, while we have a chance."

Finally, it was out there for everyone to consider, and I didn't have to be the one who raised it.

And by the looks on everyone's faces, they were considering this as well.

But the 'where' part was what I hung up on as well. Where, indeed?

And with whom? Just because we were together now didn't mean we should remain together. None of us were true family. And what bound us together in the beginning had changed.

OP's group had taken almost everything from us: our weapons, ammo, much of our gear, our vehicles, and most of our long-term supplies. We had been sustainable together with what we had, before OP's men showed up at our doorstep. But now, we were not. With the few supplies they left us, and the half of what we were growing that they allowed us to keep, we'd be out of food in a month or two at the most.

But we still didn't know where we would go. That was a huge unanswered question.

They needed to discuss this on their own. In the meantime, I had too much work to do now to participate in this useless tongue wagging. Especially in light of Joey's inadvertent comment.

"So while I'm gone, maybe you should discuss where any of us could go, and if we should split up." I turned and stomped out to the living room to get my coat. Dog sprang from the floor, always ready to follow me. I'm sure he was excited at the opportunity of going outside. I couldn't blame him; even the cold outside was better than being holed up inside, waiting for the inevitable to catch up to you.

I stopped midway and turned to the group.

Each of them were chiming in at the same time: Apparently all had thoughts on the idea of leaving, which meant they'd all had thought about this as well.

That part was good. But they all ignored the idea of splitting up, as if it had never been mentioned, and focused solely on the where. Nanette argued that they should travel down through Mexico, to where it would be warmer. Chloe weakly suggested that they should go to Southern California: Her parents were in a commune and the last she had heard, she was welcome, along with any friends. Joey said they should go to Arizona, where some of his family had a farm and had been storing up supplies for years. This idea had some merit.

Regardless of the where, I was hoping that we still had a little more time. I wasn't ready. And neither were they.

"By the way, Joey," I had to yell to get their attention. "I don't think your slip-up was that bad. Trout told us that the other group of survivalists admitted to Buster's killing. They no longer suspect us and believe us to be completely compliant to their demands. And

I'm hopeful to make a case to OP that we need more supplies. He needs me for his engine work and all of you for the fresh produce. So I think he'll back off some."

I didn't wait for a reply. I turned back to the front door, threaded my arms through my heavy jacket and slapped the side of my leg: my command for Dog to heel because we were going right then. He obeyed, as he always did.

"I'm going next door to work on one of the OP's carburetors," I announced, twisted the handle and walked through the doorway.

The three of them erupted into an argument about how cold it would be on a farm, and how it was impossible to grow anything without a greenhouse like theirs. Chloe asked if someone should check on Leticia, when I closed the door behind me.

The path I followed was not the quickest, but when traveling outside, in the snow, it was the safest, especially with the traps I'd set for anyone else who cared to try and intrude upon us. I didn't expect anyone at this point, as the cartel pretty much extinguished any competitors.

My traps were set up for the big what if: when it was time to leave. Our group knew of the traps and their locations, which I told them were set up for the wandering scavenger. I didn't tell them the real reason.

While I zipped up my parka to cut out the biting cold, I hurried my footsteps. There was a lot to do before I returned.

My old house's unlocked entrance had not been breached. That was expected, but I checked the unseen marker on the top of the door, just to be sure. Because of this, I had to put my shoulder into the door to break the icy bond which had formed, just to get it to open.

I quickly closed and locked it up and then walked directly to my basement entrance. It too was unlocked. When I opened it, Dog dashed through and down the stairs. He knew right where I was going, his big paws and nails clicking first against the wood stairs and then the basement's concrete floor.

After securing the door, I had to laugh at my procedures of dealing with the locks, as if there was anything left inside the house and the basement of value to secure. OP's men, and before them, Buster's men, had taken everything, other than the furniture. Luckily, they had left my shop equipment, only because it was so big and bulky, and they didn't know what any of it was. My shop then gave me the reason to come back to my house and do the specialized work on each of the engine parts I said I had to work on. Then I could take them back to Bob and Sarah's place—our current home—to reassemble the engine I was working on, before finally reinstalling these in OP's vehicles.

In the dark, I walked by all my equipment, without slowing.

OP's carburetors were already done. But no one had to know that or what I planned to do next.

I always doubled or tripled my estimates to allow me enough time to finish work on my own plans. And I had a lot of work ahead of me before I could leave.

Dog was seated in his place in the dark, panting, no doubt anticipating my next move.

I reached out to my steel bookcase, still full of my shop books—OP's men had no interest in these either. My hand hovered in front of the newest copy of Klymer's. I couldn't really see the book since the only light was the glare from the generator's off/on switch. I wasn't reaching for it, but I knew full well it was there. That's when a thought hit me that was so powerful, it caused me to begin weeping.

This copy, which had just arrived the day before the dam broke, was one of two proof copies I had received from the author for review. It was so new that it was certainly the last edition of this book that would ever be produced again. Every year, a new edition was produced, like the fine machinery it assessed. But this year, it would not. Nor would it ever again. My friend, the author, lived a block inland from a beach in Corpus Christi. He was washed away, like millions of others around the world.

We all suffered so many losses. But this one seemed to sting the most at that moment.

I had not shed any tears for the loss of my wife, or Sarah or Bob. People always died, and always would. I had not shed any over the loss of our weekly dinners at Anthony's. Restaurants closed all the time. I wasn't even moved by never being able to go to a store again to buy pre-packaged food—though that one should have stung pretty bad.

None of those losses caused me to lose my cool.

But it was the thought that never again would an edition of Klymer's or any other engine manual be produced. Not in my lifetime, not in anyone's.

It was all so absolute.

I could feel tears fall off my face and then splatter on the concrete below. A low moan grew from my chest.

Dog moaned back, and I could picture his head twisted at an odd angle while he studied this crazy human before him with his nocturnal eyes. I wondered what thoughts went through his dog head. And that helped me regain my composure.

I shook off the melancholy, clasped onto the bookshelf and gave it a yank. It clicked open.

When it was halfway, Dog darted through.

I ducked under the rough opening and reached for the pull-chain, clicking it on to illuminate the immediate area with a single overhead light bulb.

The small, narrow hallway-like room flooded with so much light from the sixty-watt bulb, I had to squint. I pulled on the backside of the bookcase until it clicked closed.

"No, boy," I said to Dog. He had already plopped himself on his doggy bed beside a small chair, scooted under the little table, littered with many of my notes. We weren't stopping.

A quick glance around the cramped space reminded me of the all the supplies I had to still move: 14 more cases of food, along with one case of rifles and several thousand rounds of ammo. At least 20 more trips lay ahead of us.

"Come on, Dog," I said, while slugging back the bolt in the metal exit hatch and giving a shove outward. The onrush of cold and the crashing sounds of water flooded the small chamber.

I stepped through first, then reached inside to pick up Dog. He waited patiently for me as I helped him through the opening and onto the narrow path my feet clung to.

"Damn!" I huffed, seeing that I forgot to turn off the light. I wasn't worried about anyone seeing it, only that I'd run down my battery.

I didn't want to crawl through and turn it out, when I felt the weight of each second that passed. I reached in to snag my rifle, resting by the doorway. This was slung around my back, and I stretched in the other direction to grab one of the cases of food, straining to pick it up and hoist it through the opening.

Resting it under one arm, I closed the camouflaged door, and secured it with trunk of a dead tree, which rested a foot away. It was tricky moving the heavy trunk while not dropping the case of food.

Dog woofed at me, always ready to move. And hunt. That was my deal with him, and he was good at it. With a little luck, we'd get something special for dinner.

"Dog, you're killing me. One stop first, then we hunt."

The back of my neck prickled, but I assumed it was the cold. We were both just so focused on where we were going that neither of us considered that someone was following us from behind.

CHAPTER 15

Nan

"Where's Leticia? I swear that girl disappears all the time." Chloe asked, her hands on her hips.

I looked up from the table, where I pretended to be studying my previous food calculations, acting surprised that I had barely heard Chloe's stomping procession downstairs. "She was in the 'Hole'—that's what we called the secret area where we kept our contraband, including our radio—"but I think she went to bed."

I knew Leticia was not in the Hole, because I had just looked before sitting down. She wasn't there and neither were the missing strawberry preserves.

This is what had me most concerned, not Leticia disappearing again.

Every few days more of our supplies would mysteriously disappear. At first, I wondered if my calculations were off, though each time I reran the calculations, they came out correct. But it was the strawberry preserves that cinched it. I had been specifically watching them. And when I checked and found them gone a few minutes ago, I knew one of our group had removed them between last night and this morning, before our meeting broke up when Ron left.

This was a big deal, because it meant that one of us was stealing from the rest of the group. And the repercussions of this were so huge, I just didn't want to consider this or the reason why.

Just then it occurred to me. This was Ron!

But why? Why would Ron, of all of us, steal from his own supplies, and not tell any of us?

Chloe asked something I missed, again forgetting she was there. It was something about Leticia. But at this moment, I didn't care about Leticia. I couldn't let on yet what I knew. At least not until I had a chance to directly confront Ron.

Returning my attention to Chloe, so I could get her off my back, I explained that besides escaping to the basement just before our family discussion concluded, Leticia had been down in the Hole, or at least the basement, all night. I had stopped by the basement door twice last night and could hear voices coming from the radio each time.

"This morning, I was anxious for one of her pre-recorded reports, to find out what she had learned from those broadcasts. But there was nothing left for us on the main table, or in Leticia's nook in the wall nearby... You know, where she sometimes left her recorder, all cued up and ready for us to listen?"

"Isn't it weird that she..." Chloe paused and searched for the words, "you know, barely talks to us in whole sentences—when we're like her family—but she can articulate everything so beautifully on a voice recorder?"

It was weird, but I really didn't want to discuss Leticia right now. I wanted to track down Ron next door and confront him on the missing food.

"I know..." I was going to mention the fact that what she experienced was pretty traumatic for a little girl. And that she really believed that she had some role in her parent's deaths. But I said nothing more and turned my head back to my work, hoping Chloe would get the hint and leave so I could then go and find Ron.

But Chloe continued, "Yet, that kid is obviously more brilliant than all of us put together. And—"

When my head snapped up, I must have given her the scowl of death, because she stopped mid-sentence.

"—Ah, Nan. I didn't mean anything by that. You're the smartest of all of us. I just—"

"I know what you meant," I said trying to soften my tone. "And you're right. Leticia is actually smarter than all of us, combined! At some point she'll say more than we want her to. I wouldn't worry about her. Just keep showing her the kindness you always do... Sorry, but you caught me right in the middle of calculations."

Chloe remained in her place, her eyes looking past mine, weighting one foot, and then the other. The whole Leticia conversation was just subterfuge. She was holding back asking me something else.

"Okay, so what do you want to tell me?" I asked.

"Ah shit, Nan. Am I that transparent?"

I didn't answer her.

"Okay, well, here it is. We need more fertilizer," she blurted.

"What do you mean we need more? I saw two bags there yesterday." I almost didn't believe her.

"Yeah, I thought so too. So I double-checked. And I just used the last of it. In fact, we need some right away for the new vegetable plantings we were planning for today."

"Are you sure?"

She gave a pained expression and nodded like a bobble-head.

I couldn't help but let out an enormous sigh.

Regardless of where things were going, the fertilizer had to be replaced on the double. All our lives depended on it. And it was obvious that Chloe was counting on me to do the dirty work, no matter how distasteful it was.

No time like the present.

I stood up and walked over to the battery bank, where our one radio unit was getting charged.

I yanked it out of the charger and plopped it down into the hard wood chair. Twisting the knob and glancing at the readout to make sure it was on the correct frequency, I shoved the radio to my ear and depressed the talk button.

"Base, this is Nan of the Gringos, do you hear me?" That is what they insisted we call ourselves.

I held my breath and glanced at Chloe, who was riveted.

"Si, Gringo Nan. What you want?" asked a voice I didn't recognize.

"We need four bags of fertilizer here. We just finished our last one."

I learned to ask for double what I wanted, which was double what we really needed. I only needed one for the plantings.

"Hang on Chica. Silas, he want to talk to you..."

Chloe and I gave each other the evil eye. This could not be good. Maybe Joey was right, and they put two and two together and figured it was our group that did in Buster and his clan.

"Hey Chilo, this is Silas. Don't go anywhere. We're coming to you. You have some explaining to do, so you better make sure your lies are all the same."

My stomach grumbled, as I knew we were in trouble. But I didn't know why.

"You think they're pissed about the missing supplies, or about the fact that we killed Buster?" Chloe asked.

"Yes," I said.

CHAPTER 16

Leticia

Ronald was not where he said he would be.

I needed to speak with him, because no one else seemed willing to ask him directly if he intended to leave us. I had to know, even if the other adults didn't want to.

Making sure I was not seen by anyone else, I had followed Ronald to his house.

It was easy, as he and Dog had trudged a deep path in the snow from our new home to his house. He had warned me to not venture outside, and I heard why when he told the others about the booby traps he'd laid out. So I figured following his path was safe.

The inside of his house was quiet, as expected, and very dark. This was also planned and why I brought a flashlight. I had been to Ronald's house several times, so I knew right where to look for him.

Before Polar Bear and his men found us, Ronald would let me tag along and read while he worked in his workshop. Sometimes he would even let me help him. It was then that he would tell me stories about his wife, and their times at the beach. Each time I imagined myself in his wife's place, enjoying the warm sea-breeze against my skin, hearing his laughter. It always made me smile, and somehow made everything bearable, even though daily life argued so strongly against one having any sort of joy. I missed those times.

Since Polar Bear found us, Ronald didn't let anyone follow him and he didn't talk much about the past, or anything. That was concerning enough, but then his statement earlier about whether we should "split apart" or not got to me. Added to his previous behavior, I had to wonder whether he was planning to abandon all of us.

Following his still-fresh footprints, I headed to his basement. But once through the basement doorway, which was similar to ours, I expected to hear the loud whirring of machines or Ronald speaking to Dog. Before Polar Bear, he had mostly one-way conversations with Dog, who just listened while his eyes followed Ronald as he did his thing. Now the basement was as silent as death. Even the usual soft hum of the generator was noticeably absent.

That meant there was only one place Ronald could be.

Ronald's hideaway was no secret to us. It was a small area like our Hole, where he, like us, hid things from Polar and his goons. But I had never seen his. I'm not sure any of us had seen it. Admittedly, I really wanted to see his area. It would confirm Ronald's intent by seeing what was there. And it would be easiest there to confront him about his intentions of leaving us... Leaving me.

If there was any mention of his leaving us, I would bring up the radio broadcast I had picked up again. If he knew there was a place we could all go, maybe then he wouldn't leave us.

I stopped to examine his bookshelf. Other than the books inside, it was very much like the one built by Ronald in our basement. He said he got the idea from a book of Sarah's he read about a survivalist in Mexico who hid his stash of guns and supplies behind a similar bookcase door. It sounded familiar to me as well. I reached for the latch and clicked it open.

The chamber behind this was lit, but also silent.

Stepping through, at once I found something even more disappointing than not finding Ronald and Dog where I expected them. All of the supplies.

Lining one side of the narrow chamber, stacked up higher than me, were cases of food. This was proof that it was Ronald who was taking food from our supplies and not telling anyone. Nan said that some of the supplies seemed to be mysteriously disappearing, forcing her to recount them more than once.

It felt like a slap across my face. I wanted to scream.

Something else was wrong, or rather out of place.

There was dirt, leaves and moisture at the far end of the chamber, when there should be none. Additionally, its concrete wall was covered in a camouflage netting that we didn't have in our secret chamber. Ours was obscured by a life-sized poster board of a book cover. It didn't make any sense, unless...

Until you stood up to the netting, it was impossible to know the space behind it was empty. I reached through the netting, driving my hand deep inside. At my shoulder, I felt an ice-cold but smooth lever, attached to a solid metal wall. I leaned into the mesh, my face pressed into it and gave the latch a twisting yank downward, causing a clank.

The whole wall moved.

A burst of frigid air blew the netting around me and that's when it all made sense.

Casting the netting aside revealed a roughly hewn hole in the concrete wall, with the metal door behind it. Ronald had jackhammered the hole and installed a heavy metal door to the outside, without telling a soul. But why?

When Nan was convalescing, she asked me several times what the rumbling was under the floor. She was convinced it was more earthquakes like those that destroyed many of the houses around us and damaging our house and Ronald's house.

The horror of it all clicked in.

Ronald had been planning this long ago, at least more than a month ago. But why would he lie about this and pretend that he was staying, unless he was planning to leave the whole time?

Like a cold blanket, anger like what I felt when Buster killed my parents in front of me covered me. And my heart felt shattered into a million pieces.

I felt betrayed and wanted him to tell me why he was going to do this, no matter how much it hurt.

I pushed at the metal door, ignoring the strong gust of wind and harsh sounds of a river attempting to send me in the other direction. My eyes watered, but not just from the cold.

A large tree trunk slid past the opening and thunked to the ground below, startling me.

I hoisted myself up and through the opening in the concrete and lowered my feet onto the log that had fallen. I had to push the hatch open some more to wiggle my way out. I turned and put my back to an outside earthen wall and took in my surroundings.

It was the area right below Ronald's property, near where he had set up the wheel in the river to generate electricity for our batteries.

Below me was a path that led down to and along the riverbank. I could see Ronald's and Dog's tracks leading away.

For a moment, I wondered if I should turn around and tell the others about this now, or continue following their path to wherever it led. Much of me did not want to be disappointed any further. But I had to know.

I gave the door a stiff push, so that it was closed, and found the corresponding latch on the outside. A twist of this generated an opposite clunk sound inside, indicating that it was secured.

Taking a step back, I couldn't help but appreciate the work he put into it. It was quite ingenious, as Ronald had rigged up natural moss and tree branches to cover the door. And when I stepped away from it, other than the tracks leading to it, there was no evidence of a doorway. Unless you were looking for one.

I turned to the footprints and followed them, planting each of my smaller boots inside each of his prints.

Just before the river, I stopped in my tracks, or rather his.

Ronald and Dog had turned at a T and headed away, along a path I had seen before, which followed the river. But at the turn, there was another set of tracks. These too were boot prints, and almost a carbon copy of Ronald's. They were fresher too. These prints continued beside Ronald's and Dog's.

Someone was following them.

CHAPTER 17

Ron

The food felt twice as heavy as normal, and I racked my brains over how I would get the rest of the food to its final hiding place before it was time to go. I figured I had maybe one or two days, max, before I'd have to report back to Polar. Then I would be ready to go.

There was just too much to do before then.

When I had lost the sound of Dog, who had long since darted ahead, I called out, "Dog. Come on, boy!"

An excited woof, muffled by distance, responded.

The case of food found its way onto the other shoulder, and I trudged forward, calling out Dog's name—or rather, the non-name that he had inherited from me.

He burst through an opening in the trees, the same place I was headed. Something dead hung out of his mug.

"What did you bring us, Dog?" I belted out, excited for him.

Dog jumped into the air in celebration of his kill. He let out a muffled woof, which probably meant, "Look what I got, Papa," in Dog lingo. I did something I hadn't done in a while. I giggled.

How could you not feel some joy just looking at him? He was in seventh heaven in the woods and snow. He loved snuffing the stuff and bouncing around like a child high after emptying a bag of gummy bears. But even more than playing in the snow, Dog loved to hunt.

This time, he got a fox—a good-sized one by the look of it. It was going to make a nice little meal tonight. I couldn't wait to see what Nanette was going to do with it.

Dog dropped his prize and awaited his praise.

"What a good dog! Come on boy, we have to get this stuff packed away. We can celebrate later."

As if he seemed to understand everything, Dog grabbed the neck of the dead animal and paraded in front of me, all the way to our destination.

Perhaps it was knowing how much more work lay ahead of me, but by the time I made my way around the warehouse to the front I was exhausted.

Getting the key out of my pocket was easy enough. But before I could use it to unlock the front door, I almost lost the case of food. When I finally released the door, I was already accepting my defeat. I just wouldn't be able to get everything done that I had planned. "It's just too much for one person," I grunted to Dog.

Dog woofed back, either to tell me that there were in fact two people here, or to tell me that he wanted inside.

I pushed open the door and Dog slipped in. It was his job to make sure we didn't have any visitors lurking. Before the apocalypse, I would not have expected another soul out there, mainly because it is so far off the beaten path and so well hidden. When I heard no other sounds but from Dog snuffing the cobwebs, I ducked in.

The case of food made its way on top of the others in the back of the old truck bed. A quick glance in the bed and then the cab confirmed what I remembered: There was barely enough room for Dog and me up front, in the cab, much less room for more food there or in the truck bed. It was more than we needed, but I figured the extras could always be used for barter. Perhaps we were good with what we had.

Dog barked out a warning, and I swung around to look and see what he wanted.

He was focused on the back of the building, so I clicked on my flashlight and trained it on the corner.

The trees moved outside, framed by the tiny back window, like wispy ghosts doing a jig. No threats.

I glanced once more at the truck. I made the decision then that I'd go back and get one or maybe two more cases before I'd call it quits for the day. Then I could get the rest I needed, long before I saw OP and his men again. That would give me enough time to lay out the last part of my plan before leaving.

Only then would I be free from that lunatic mass-murderer, who would just as soon kill you because you spoke up before being invited. Free of the constant beatings by his men, who hated the attention OP showed me because of my unique skills. I now hung my hope on using those skills to find my way out of this.

Soon, I told myself.

"Come on, Dog. Let's go back."

I think because I had made this trip so many times over the past month, I must have been absent-minded and didn't pay attention to what was going on around me.

I certainly didn't expect any more stragglers or people wandering along this stretch of creek. Once again, I was lulled into a sense of comfort. Which was stupid.

But when I distinctly heard the noise in back and Dog dropped the fox from his mug and growled, I knew I should have been paying better attention.

I flicked off the safety from my rifle and swung it around to where Dog was pointed.

Then I heard the thump-thump-thump of running feet.

Someone had followed us here.

❄ ❄ ❄

Leticia

When the two sets of footsteps turned into one, I really worried about Ronald's safety.

But then it appeared like the other set—the one following Ronald—disappeared. Now it was just Ronald's tracks and the faint prints of Dog in and around Ronald's.

I spun around, expecting to see the other person lurking about, but didn't see anyone. Just thinking about this made the hairs on the back of my neck stand at attention.

The wind whipped through the trees, creating eerie sounds all around. But none of them were manmade.

Simple. I must have missed them somewhere. More important was to get to Ronald. So I returned to his tracks until I found myself at a mostly hidden rectangular building, surrounded by snow-covered debris. This was another one of Ron's surprises.

His footprints made their way around the building, to what must have been the front. But that's not where I decided to go.

Nested in the back corner of the building was a little window which momentarily flashed a beam of light, like from a flashlight.

Below it was a metal barrel that I knew I could use to boost myself up and onto, then stand on to peek inside.

I did a quick look around. Not seeing a soul, I jumped up and onto the barrel and cupped my hands around my eyes and pressed my face against the window to see through it. There he was.

Ronald was moving something into the back of a good-sized pickup truck. It was completely filled with what looked like supplies: food, big bottles of water, and other things. He pulled a tarp over the truck bed but didn't tie it off, probably because he expected to add more to it.

Dog was just inside the doorway, very visible in the light. Dog barked—I could hear him too—and Ronald spun around and pointed his flashlight in my direction.

I sank below the window.

Having seen more than enough evidence—all the supplies that were missing; a pickup truck with only two open spaces in front, barely enough for him and Dog, but no more; and then there was all the secrecy—it was obvious what he intended to do.

He was going to leave us!

I felt heartbroken and leapt from the barrel to the ground, making a crashing sound behind me. I didn't care. I ran, intending to tell Nanette and everyone what Ronald was planning to do to me... to us.

I wasn't watching where I was going. My mind was focused on the hurt and the desire to just get back, when I ran into a tree-sized man who stood like an impenetrable wall in front of me.

His giant mitt-like hands snatched me before I could react.

"Where you are going in such a hurry, chiquita?" the man said in a voice that sounded smaller than his hands.

I glared up at his giant mug, a smile sneaking out of his dirty grey beard. Based on the way he was dressed, it was one of Mr. Polar's men. And he was armed with a scary-looking rifle.

"That's okay. We go and ask your friend and see if he answer why you in a hurry. He and I are old friends."

CHAPTER 18

Nan

I practically ran to Ron's basement workshop next door.

It was colder than yesterday; the wicked wind thrashed me sideways, almost knocking me over. I barely noticed.

My heart beat rapid-fire, as I knew we had little time to decide what to do. Trout and his men were coming very soon, to confront us.

He had said, "...you better make sure your lies are all the same."

They had caught us lying about something. But what?

Would he have said that if he knew that one of us had killed Polar's son, Buster? Maybe not. But if not that, what?

I was frantic to find Ron and figure out our next move. The missing supplies were barely a concern now.

Ron's front door opened easily, as I would have expected since he had already been there. After a day, the outside door locks froze up and you really had to lean into the door with a shoulder to get the damned thing to budge sometimes, unless someone had done this just before you. Ron's door was the worst.

Boot tracks on his carpet revealed his trail right to the basement door.

I clicked on my flashlight—we all carried these now, but we were careful to use them only when needed to maintain our batteries—and opened his basement door.

Stopping at the head of the stairs, I listened, expecting to hear either Ron or Dog or even Leticia speaking. But it was quiet. Way too quiet.

"Hello? Is anyone down here?" I yelled, mostly for my own safety.

After not hearing a reply, I marched down the stairs, but stopped halfway. There were beads of water and even a little sleet on the stairs, which meant that either Ron or Dog or Leticia had tracked in some of the snow within the last few minutes. There was only one place they could be.

Ron had created hiding places in both basements, mostly for our protection—sort of a safe room if our houses were invaded. But it was also for hiding supplies from intruders. Later, these became vital hiding spots for our supplies and weapons which were not already confiscated by Polar's men.

Ron said he got the idea from a science fiction book where the main prepper, who lived on a Mexico beach, had a secret hiding place behind a bookcase.

In Ron's case, this bookcase held all of his mechanical and engine books.

I reached behind the farthest book on the top-most shelf and found the latch. As I gave it a pull, the bookcase clicked and then moved slightly.

Giving it a yank, I pulled it open and glanced in the safe room, already lit by the single overhead bulb.

I expected to see the three of them reading or in quiet conversation, but there was no one there. Just a large stack of our missing supplies.

Actually, it was just some of our missing supplies. There were other cases of food, and guns and ammo missing. But a fair amount of what was missing was right there. In Ron's secret room.

It was like a gut punch.

Ron had been quietly taking supplies for a few weeks now and said nothing. Even when I asked him directly how my calculations could be wrong, he said nothing.

I was tired of his secrets. And the lies.

Now I was more frightened than ever. Lingering in the back of my mind was a kernel of a thought that made me shiver: What if Ron was leaving us, and what if he left already to deal with Polar and his men alone?

I don't even remember leaving the basement. I just remember dashing out his front door and running, not sure where I would go. I ran as fast as I could to the house. My thinking was that I would grab Joey and Chloe and we would run down to the river.

It wasn't much of a plan, but all I knew was that Ron was not anywhere to help us and we might have to leave now.

When I made it to front of the property, I stopped dead in my tracks.

In between the two houses, was Chloe.

She was standing hunched over, with her palms pushed out, her face twisted pretzel-like, in terror.

Only a few feet from her was a huge wolf.

CHAPTER 19

Ron

My rifle led our way.

The movement on the other side of the window was from the trees being racked by the wind. But the sound of the spare barrel in back thumping to the ground and subsequent footfalls scurrying away made it obvious. Someone had followed me.

Either this was one of Polar's men or some transient who should not have been alive, much less spying on me. Neither were good options. All I needed was just one more day, maybe two, to complete my preparations. Then I was ready. Anyone who had seen what I was doing would interrupt my plans before then. So regardless of who it was, I had to find and silence this intruder before it was too late.

Dog was commanded to trail behind me, as I wanted to move rapidly to catch whomever it was. But if my target somehow got around me, Dog would have our backs.

The footprints were pronounced, the person not caring about being tracked. But then it struck me that this person was very small. I had met a couple of Polar's men who were small, but not this small.

It didn't really matter. Polar's man or not, I couldn't let this person go. Even if it was some transient who accidentally stumbled upon me and my hidden garage, I had no choice. Either way, my hidden supplies were now known and would be taken. And with them, my exit plan. I knew what I had to do. And this caused my gut to rumble. I couldn't hold them hostage: Leaving someone tied up or injured would be a death warrant out here anyway. I would have to kill another man.

A worse thought struck me like a lightning bolt. What if it was a woman?

Could I kill a woman, just to protect my secret?

Before I could resolve this moral quandary, I halted when I heard the crack of branches, followed by the unmistakable sounds of footsteps. The intruder was approaching.

I glanced back but didn't see Dog.

In front of me, the footsteps grew louder, along with another sound.

Sniffling.

I aimed my rifle at the point I expected this person to come out from the trees. Based on the prints, I was aiming chest high.

Another branch cracked just a few feet away.

My finger hovered over the trigger, and I felt sweat drip down my sides from my soaked armpits.

A familiar face, not a chest, appeared in my sights.

It was Leticia. She was my intruder?

I lowered my rifle, but then raised it up again in one swift motion and let my finger slip back on the trigger.

This time I aimed higher.

A short man, who was as wide as a 100-year-old oak tree, held an AK-47 pistol against the back of Leticia's head, only a couple of feet behind her. I had a clean shot, but if I did, he would shoot her.

Leticia's eyes were swollen, her cheeks puffy and red.

"Better stop, Gringo," commanded Oak Tree. "Unless you want this chiquita's head to explode."

I removed my finger from the trigger and held out a palm to indicate I wasn't going to shoot.

"Drop the gun," he commanded, stepping more into my view. "Or I will shoot your little friend."

With snail-like motions, I lowered my rifle, all the while keeping my eyes glued to this man. The man looked so familiar.

His serious scowl, set across skin only a shade or two lighter than Leticia's, started to form a smile. He wore a white camo winter outfit, indicating that he belonged to OP. He must have been assigned to watch us.

With each inch that my gun was lowered, my heart sank even more. The cold realization that we were done stabbed at me like icicles. They had us dead to rights. With this man, they probably knew all of our hiding spots. And that meant they would have our secret stash of supplies. More than anything, he knew we were lying to OP.

We would not survive this... Unless...

Nestled in my pocket was a quick-release hunting knife. If somehow I could get to it and get Oak Tree to come to me, maybe...

"Now step away," the man demanded. He snapped a look back and then returned his scowl to me. "No one coming from behind to save you this time."

Then I knew. This was the man I encountered outside of OP's compound. The one Joey had clobbered on the back of the head. He wouldn't fall for my ruse easily.

I took an exaggerated step back and didn't have to exaggerate what happened next. I tumbled backwards, screaming "Ahhh!" as I hit hard, expelling a loud grunt when I came to rest.

"Ughhh," I groaned, my knife already out of my pocket and slowly being clicked into place.

Now, if he'd only get close enough.

❄ ❄ ❄

Nan

The wolf pawed its way closer to Chloe, its teeth exposed and terrifying. It growled viciously at her and I knew then if I didn't do something quick, the wolf would attack her and that would be it.

"Oh God, Nan, pleassssse..." Her voice was many octaves higher than normal, but it came out barely above a whisper.

I wasn't armed, and at best, if Chloe even remembered to grab it, she only had that stupid little .38-stubby. But she did not have it out. Even if she weren't too petrified to pull it out, she wasn't likely to be able to aim and shoot the animal. We are screwed.

"Hey!" I yelled as loudly as I could muster, my breath a billow of white steam.

The wolf halted and turned to me, glaring a warning to stay back, but not at all frightened.

"Chloe, do you have the pistol with you?"

She shuddered and barely turned her head enough for me to see her mouth "no." She didn't dare speak.

I pulled my radio out and in one motion, I twisted the volume to max and hit the call button, making it blare out a cruelly loud tone. Bawwwwwwww!

The animal barely flinched. Then it resumed its attention on its prey, Chloe.

"Nooooo," she whimpered.

The useless radio would have to have another use.

"Okay, Chloe." I took a loud step in their direction, and the wolf turned back to me. "I'm going to get the wolf off you, but the moment I do, run to the house and get Joey or a weapon. Okay?"

No answer.

"Chloe, dammit! Okay?" I hollered.

She nodded.

Taking one more heavy step forward, I tugged at my thick scarf until it was free from my neck and wrapped it around my left forearm. I knew it wouldn't be of much use, but I was out of choices.

I took a breath and said, "Okay, you sonofabitch." And I charged it.

CHAPTER 20

Ron

"Get up!" threatened Oak Tree.

"Oh, shit," I said. I was lying on my side, clutching my ankle with my free hand. "Ahhhh... I think I broke something," I groaned. My head was half buried in the snow, my right side already prickling from the cold. My eyes had been shut since I had exaggerated my fall. But now I peeked out my left to see what he'd do next.

"I not fall for any more of your tricks," Oak Tree said with swagger and walked over to my rifle, reaching down to pick it up. Oak Tree had forgotten about little Leticia, who darted away from him and out of sight before the big man could even react.

He swung around in her direction, spitting out something in Spanish, before returning his attention to me. I drilled my eye shut when he spun back around to face me and huffed, "Little Chiquita abandoned you. It's just you and me now. Get up."

My eyes remained shut, because I could hear his movements in the snow, and I wanted him to think I was really hurt. I groaned some more for good measure and then said, "I think I broke something serious."

Oak Tree took a lumbering step closer and then another. "If I have to make you move, I not happy. OP already going to be angry with you for you sneaking around, rather than doing your jobs for him..."

Oak took another step closer and was maybe a foot or two away. I could hear his labored breathing.

My heart raced, but I wasn't scared. There was only one option for us: I had to stop this man, even if it killed me. But this had to happen soon, as I was losing feeling in my right side from the cold. I groaned some more.

"That's it," Oak huffed, and clasped his mitt to my left forearm.

Now!

I flicked open my eyes, rolled over onto his hand, pulling him closer, and swung around with my right arm, my knife in hand and fully extended.

The big man let go of me and took a step backward.

My hand arced around to where his neck was supposed to be, missing him entirely.

Oak took another step back. "I warned you," he said.

He swung his AK-47 back in my direction.

❄ ❄ ❄

Nan

The wolf turned his full attention to me now.

I didn't have a real plan. It was a damned wolf, after all, with teeth and claws. And all I had was a radio and a flashlight. But it was a special flashlight.

Ronald had secretly given it to me, as OP's men took all the good ones. It was a little larger than my hand, and had points on its front. He said it was for self-defense.

So I ran full steam at the wolf, yelling profanities at it, leading with my wrapped left forearm holding the radio, and the flashlight clutched in my right like a knife.

The wolf growled at me and then sprang. In two fluid strides, he was upon me.

Just before he struck, I tripped.

I swung my right arm around, expecting to stab the beast right in front of my wrapped arm, but then I was headed to the ground face-first.

I felt my right hand connect with something solid, jarring my whole body and spinning me around at an odd angle.

First, I was looking at the ground, and then I was upside down, staring at the sky as the wolf flashed past me.

I landed hard, looked up and saw that the wolf had landed in a clumsy fashion too. It rolled around and was readying itself to attack again. But I wasn't going to be able to do anything this time.

My right arm, already damaged from the impact, lay beneath my body. And I lost the radio.

I struggled to get it free, when the wolf took a bounding leap in my direction. My scarf-wrapped arm raised futilely, and I braced for its impact.

The wolf, barely another leap away, dipped down, folding its legs for the final spring.

Ba-ba-ba-ba-boom!

❄ ❄ ❄

Ron

Oak Tree's eyes locked into mine, and I could tell he was going to kill me now.

He smiled at this, obviously taking satisfaction in my knowing I was done for.

Pop-pop-pop-pop-pop echoed rapid-fire gun shots.

I shuddered at first, thinking it was Oak, but then realized they came from nearby, not from him.

Oak glanced in that direction and then returned his gaze to me.

"You next, Gring—"

A flash of brownish fur hit one of Oak's arms, knocking him down before he could finish.

Dog!

I had wondered where he went.

Oak landed on the ground, but recovered quickly, even though Dog was attached to him and shook wildly.

Oak got onto a knee and reached for his AK.

I leapt at him, my knife still firmly clutched in my hand.

Oak grabbed his rifle at the moment I came down on him, this time connecting with his other arm. And before he could recover, I stabbed at him again.

And again.

CHAPTER 21

Ron

The massive shot of adrenalin had worn off when I thought about giving up.

Immediately after my battle with Oak Tree, I hurt, my gut wanted to extricate my meager breakfast, and I was physically spent. Then I remembered the gunshots and thinking they weren't from Chloe's .38 snubby or Joey's .22 rifle, and that meant one of OP's men had fired the shots.

As much as I wanted to run to the gunshots, because surely one of our own was hurt, I just couldn't leave the body of one of OP's men to be found.

So, with growing fear of what carnage awaited me at our home, and what little energy I had left, I pulled Oak Tree—who also weighed as much as an oak—into the river.

That was a trial in itself as most of the river's water was frozen over already.

I had to pull the body onto the ice. Then, lying prone on its cold surface, I used my rifle and feet to nudge him closer to the middle, until the surface cracked, and he slipped through. I lay there, watching the man I killed get consumed by the Guadalupe and I almost felt envious of him.

The man no longer suffered the physical and emotional pains of life. He no longer worried about other people. He was free.

I felt myself letting go then. My eyes shut and I could picture Liz's face. Her glorious smile warmed my frozen insides. I should have joined her almost six months ago. I could easily join her now if I just let go.

"Ronald," she said to me.

"Ronald, are-are you alive," a stuttering voice barely called out, almost imperceptibly.

It wasn't Liz.

My eyes flicked open, and with them, the cold, and the pain, and the torment returned.

"Ronald?" whimpered the little voice behind me.

I rolled around and glanced up at Leticia. Like a little shivering mummy, wrapped up in winter clothing, arms folded around her chest, she stood at the edge of the riverbank glowering at me, tears streaming down her face. Dog sat patiently beside her, staring at me expectantly.

Rather than relief at seeing I was alive, her face seized up. I understood why.

It was all the blood. There was a trail of it leading from the bank, where she stood, to me. And I was covered in it. But I was sure it was all Oak Tree's and not my own.

"I'm fine." The memory of the sounds of the gunshots moments ago gave me urgency again. "Come on, let's get back."

She nodded and then shuddered again. Her head spun, as if on a swivel. "But what about..." She must not have seen what I had done with the body or figured out whose blood this was.

"Don't worry, Leticia. He won't hurt us again."

Everything that followed was a blur, except for one part.

After collecting Oak Tree's gun and slinging it and my rifle over a shoulder, I tried to massage my tender ankle and other frozen parts back into working order. Leticia's shock must have left her, as she did something completely unexpected. She proceeded to tell me in one long, rapid-fire sentence about her escape.

How she had fled from Oak Tree's grasp, to run and tell Nanette and the others. But then she'd changed her mind, because there wouldn't be time, and then she heard the gunshots. So she returned to help me. Then she saw all the blood, the drag marks and then me lying on the ice.

After I further reassured her that I wasn't seriously injured and that I wasn't going anywhere—she asked me three times—the three of us returned to the house. It took forever coming up from the river, as I had a profound limp from my ankle twisting. We all halted, catching our breaths in our throats, when I got my next course of adrenalin for the afternoon.

There was blood in an area of the snow where there was a lot of activity. Right next to the blood was Nanette's flashlight.

Admittedly, I had to gulp back the bile. My head pounded as well, as I tried to process what I was looking at.

Then I saw the fur and realized that the gore didn't appear to have come from a human. It also told me that the shots were probably fired at one of the wolves Chloe had spoken about earlier. Nanette must have been there and dropped her flashlight.

I leaned over, picked it up, and put it in my pocket, while considering what this meant.

"Is Nanette okay?" Leticia asked.

"I think so," I whispered. "Grab hold of Dog's collar and follow behind me quietly."

Leticia didn't respond, but she did as I asked and lightly took hold of Dog's collar in a hand. They followed me from behind as I led us to our shared home along the garage side. I stopped at the corner, took a breath, and then peaked out around it to see what awaited us.

Parked in front of the house was one of OP's previously unused H2 Hummers. I had looked it over last week and told them it was okay to use. The man in the driver's seat gazed forward, right at us, but also looked bored.

I backed up out of sight before he spotted me. I knew what I had to do.

"Hold tightly onto Dog and don't move. I'll be right back."

Leticia gave me a glassy-eyed look like she didn't believe me.

I dashed straight back the way we had come, this time stopping before the trail declined down to the river. There was a berm at the end of my property that was a dirt pile of fill that I never had time to use. Then the ash fell and then snow, covering it and everything else up.

Halfway down the trail, after passing a deadfall of bushes, I trudged across and then back up a steep grade of weeds off the trail, so that my tracks weren't obvious. Once at the back of the berm, I took off my bloodied coat and gloves, wrapped them around my rifle and Oak Tree's AK and pressed this bundle into the snow, so they were not visible to anyone walking around the back property. Leaning in, I grabbed a branch and yanked it from one of the trees. Only a few strokes of the branch was all it took to smooth the snow into something more natural looking.

When satisfied, I made my way back to Leticia.

We had the conversation again about not letting go of Dog. As long as she held his collar, Dog would never leave Leticia's side. If she did let go... Well, let's say I pity the person Dog had his sights on at that point.

Together, the three of us walked around the corner of the garage to the front of the house.

The Hummer driver became alert immediately. He fumbled with his door, practically falling out of it. He collected himself and was about to dash forward and get into our faces but stopped like a frozen totem when he saw Dog.

We ignored him and marched past, not knowing what awaited us inside.

We walked through the front door, my heart crashing in my chest, but I acted—as best I could—like we had just returned from a leisurely walk.

As soon as Dog entered with Leticia, he growled. "It's all right, I got him," I said to Leticia, who let go and then slunk behind both of us as we entered. Dog was my only weapon, if I needed him, and I wanted to make sure the intruders knew I had some control.

The first ugly mug I saw was Matador's, who was standing on the other side of the door, an M4 rifle slung forward. He wore his usual untouchable smirk. And with both hands on his weapon, it was obvious he wanted the opportunity to use it. But fear only hit me when I gazed into the living room.

Nanette, Chloe and Joey were parked beside each other on the living room couch. Nanette was clutching a wrapped-up hand, looking at first like she might jump out of her skin and then letting out a huge sigh. Chloe was shaking like a leaf in an Arctic gale. Joey appeared emasculated and small. Defeated. And standing beside them was Trout, with a stern gaze, focused right at me.

"Oh, finally the prodigal son returns," he said. "You missed the big show," he continued.

CHAPTER 22

Nan

When Ron, Leticia and Dog finally showed up, I was ready to crawl out of my skin.

Trout had had all of us sitting and waiting for Ron and, as Trout said, "that dumb kid and her crazy mutt," before he would tell us what we did wrong. I had assured Trout that Ron would be back from working on OP's engine or the turbine, but I wasn't so sure anymore.

When they first arrived, I was so relieved at their safe return, I don't even remember what Trout said to them. Ron had some blood on him, but there weren't any obvious wounds. What was obvious was that he was no longer wearing a winter coat.

Trout glared at Ron. "So you were down by the river fixing a turbine that was freezing. You didn't see another man when you were out there, did you?"

When Ron just furrowed his brow without giving any other response, Trout continued, "You couldn't miss him. Fat and short, with skin as dark as the kid's. His only job was sticking close to you, without you knowing it. And he does his job really good."

My heart raced again. What had OP's short spy seen? How long had he been watching Ron?

Ron shook his head. "No!" He shrugged his shoulders as if to say he really didn't know.

"And I suppose you don't know how that blood got on you either?"

Ron pretended to examine his hands for the blood, then his pant legs, where several small dots of brownish red were mostly hidden by the dirt on his jeans. He nodded, as if figuring out this puzzle. "It's from the fox that Dog hunted and caught."

"And where is that fox?"

"Ah, I guess I left it hanging in a tree when I came running toward the gunshots."

"It doesn't look like you were too out of breath if you were running."

"That's because I stopped for a while to figure out that it was a wolf that someone had shot, and not someone I cared about."

Trout's glare intensified when Ron said this, either because of his "someone I cared about" comment or because he didn't believe any of Ron's answers. I was downright frightened by Trout's line of questioning. I felt flushed and overheated. For a moment, I thought I might pass out.

"Okay, so I guess I don't need to tell you what happened then, since you already know everything," Trout huffed. "We'll see how you stand up to Polar Bear's questioning next. And I will tell you, he is not happy with you, amigo. So let's get down to business."

Trout must have signaled something to Matador, because the disgusting man flashed a rotten smile and made a move toward Ron.

"First," Trout said, brandishing his pistol at Joey, "hand over the two peashooters we gave you."

Matador jammed the barrel of his rifle hard into the square of Ron's back, almost knocking him down.

"Whoa!" Joey belted. "The rifle is in the kitchen, and you know that."

"So where's the pistol?" Matador demanded.

"Chloe," I said in a reassuring voice, "do you have that on you, dear, or did you leave it somewhere?"

Chloe snapped at this, as if she had been slapped. Then realization hit her. She shoved a hand in her coat pocket and pulled out the .38. She had it her the whole time, as I had suspected.

"Don't move, Chiquita," Matador yelled.

Chloe jumped again, dropping the gun in between us on the couch.

"Stay where you are," Matador demanded, as he shuffled over and ran his hand in between both of us, while staring at Chloe.

Joey attempted to stand up, but Trout pushed him down. I grabbed Matador's wrist, stopping him from exploring further. "You're done. You've got the weapon," I said.

He poured out a look of hatred at me. With reeking breath, he said, "Señora, I'll say when I'm done. And I just start—"

"So"—Trout cut in—"here's how things are going to go from here on out. Matador will be living here for the next couple of days, to learn how you run your garden growing operation. He wants to run this from our mota building."

Chloe's head nearly spun off her neck as she whipped it around toward Trout and then back to Matador and then to Joey. Her shaking almost looked like epileptic convulsions.

Trout snatched the .38 from Matador. "So you don't need your weapons now, because Matador will protect you as long as we need him to.

"Finally, Mr. Ash will be coming with me to answer for what he's done. Come on." Trout walked toward Ron. "Give the mutt to the kid and we go now." Trout stopped at the door, opened it up, and a whoosh of wind and snow blew in.

It was then that I caught a glimpse of a familiar black fabric bag Trout had slung over his far shoulder. But before it even registered, he and the bag were out of sight.

Dog, who had been in a low growl and baring his teeth the whole time, reacted to Ron leaving by whining.

Ron gave Dog a quick pet. Then he gazed at me and mouthed "It's okay," turned and walked out the door. I feared it was the last time we'd ever see him.

When the door closed, Dog turned on his growl and focused his attention on Matador. This caused Matador to blare at Leticia, who was holding tight to Dog's collar with both hands, "And I expect you to stay in your room with that chuchó rabioso while I'm here, or I'll shoot both of you. Comprende?"

Dog's growl grew more vicious, no doubt because he was called a 'rabid mutt.' More so, it was Dog's reminder of who was really the alpha here.

Matador took a step back and pointed his rifle at Dog. "Do you understand, or are you as stupid as you look?"

I'd not seen anger in Leticia before, just frustration. At this question, her face tightened, and her lips quivered. But she remained silent. I wondered if she was trying to figure out how to release Dog on this man without Dog getting shot.

And for a moment, I almost helped her, by creating a diversion. But I did nothing, again.

Finally, Leticia said, "Come on, Dog. This paragon of the English language has nothing else interesting to say." And they both left.

When I snickered at Leticia's jab, Matador spun around to address us on the couch. He leered at Chloe and then stated, "Well, well. Looks like I'm going to spend a little time with you muchachas."

Joey sprang up from his seat and stood in between Matador and Chloe. "And I'll be right here to assist you." He turned his head away from Matador. "Chloe, get into the greenhouse so we can show this man what we do."

"Actually," Matador squared his shoulders to Joey, "I will decide who I learn from, and I say her." He pointed at where Chloe was, but she was already out of sight.

"Look." Joey took a step back and dropped his shoulders. "We all know you're the badass with the gun, but we want to make ourselves useful to OP. Tell us what you need from us."

Matador seemed unsure what to do next. He obviously wasn't supposed to shoot us, at least not yet, because he would have shot Joey at that moment to show his dominance. And I had no doubt, from Trout's earlier comments, that he had done this many times.

Then it was as if the man didn't have a single idea in his head and one popped in at that moment. "Ah, Trout wants you to show me first exactly where all the garden supplies are. Then I... You can teach me."

"What do they want with Ron?" I asked.

"OP has a score to settle with your man. Nothing you can do about that. Your only worry right now is making me happy."

CHAPTER 23

Leticia

Yes, that man was beyond creepy. But I was not running away from him.

I was now more determined than ever to find a sanctuary for us. Then Ronald would somehow get free, like he always did—he was like one of those indestructible, can-do-everything spies in my novels. Then he would come back to save us, kill all the bad men, and I would persuade him to leave with us to the perfect place I had found, where we could all live in peace, away from bad men.

When Dog and I were through the doorway, I clasped my hand around the doorknob and put my whole body into slamming the basement door behind me. Yes, it was a bit passive-aggressive on my part. But if it's okay for adults to do this all the time, why not me?

A quick twist at the handle and the door lock was engaged. It would do little to keep the Matador out. But this would give Dog and me some time to cover up what we were about to do if OP's man wanted to come down.

"Come on, Dog, let's do some exploring together."

The world's smartest dog led the way, practically galloping down the stairs. At the floor, he slid into his turn and then he tore out of sight. A couple of seconds later, he woofed his arrival, letting the slowpoke human —that's me—know he wanted me to hurry.

He was practically whining when I arrived at the secret bookcase.

You can call me paranoid or stupid, but after Trout's comment about the fat man following Ron around, I looked around me just to make sure no one was hiding down there. Only after confirming the obvious did I unlatch the bookshelf opening.

Dog darted in first. I'd like to think this was to ease my paranoia, by his checking out the room to prove there were no bad guys lurking in there too.

I knew better.

The opening was low even for me. So I ducked slightly to walk in, leaving the bookshelf door open so we could hear if someone wanted in from above. A click on the chain ignited the room in white light from the single bulb dangling from the ceiling.

Dog was seated on the concrete, near the table—about midway in the room—slugging a paw in the air, like he was scratching at something above the floor that only his doggie eyes could see.

"Okay, Dog. You are such a good boy," I said, mimicking what Ron did in these circumstances. A few feet away was a gallon-sized Ziploc baggie with dog treats. Dog could have certainly ripped it open and helped himself to the entire contents, but he was too much of a gentleman to do so. I opened the bag and snatched two of them.

With my free hand, I shook his levitated paw and gave both to him with my other. He scarfed up both in one breath. Then, satisfied with his double treat, he scurried back to the entrance, where his small bed lay.

He grumpfed as he plopped into it.

"Okay, Dog. You let me know if you hear someone coming our way. Okay?"

Dog groaned and laid his face on the edge of his bedding and closed his eyes. That was Dog for I got this, girlfriend!

I sat down at the table, turned on the radio and plugged in the headset. Pressing one side of the headphones to my right ear, I turned up the volume and twirled the control knob to the frequency had I last heard them on.

Of course, there was nothing. And even though I knew the chance of my reaching anyone was slim, I figured, What the heck?

I pulled the microphone over and clicked the red button. "CQ, CQ, CQ"—this amateur radio code for calling any fellow amateur radioists or anyone who can hear me—"This is WB9ZMO, Whiskey Bravo Nine Zulu Mike Oscar, calling for anyone listening on this channel." I let go of the mic button and listened for a response that I knew wouldn't come.

There was no doubt in my mind that the dipole wire-antenna I had measured out and Ron had erected for me would get my signal out there. I just doubted there were many people still alive who also had workable ham radio gear and the batteries to power it, and who were listening. But there was one. So I called again, like I had for weeks now, just in case they were there.

I realized at that moment that I had forgotten to record this. I needed my recorder and the proper SD card to record the signal, just in case they answered. The logbook was also with my recorder in my bag... On the opposite side of the basement.

I looked at Dog, wishing he could get it for me, but that was asking too much, even for the world's smartest dog.

The radio's static blared out of the tiny speaker when I swapped out the headset plug. A quick rotation of the volume control brought it down to a low enough level that I could still hear it, without uninvited ears from above catching anything.

"I'm coming right back, Dog," I said as I ducked under the opening and marched to the table everyone uses in this otherwise nearly empty basement.

Once at the table, I looked up at the stairwell, concentrating on the potential sound of someone coming our way, while I blindly reached for my bag, which contained my recorder, about 200 SD cards, the logbook, and my story notebook.

The space was empty.

I spun around and glared at the empty space where my bag always lay, because Ron asked me not to carry it around anymore out of his fear. He figured if I dropped it, what was on my records would hurt all of us if found by anyone else, especially OP and his men. I was instructed to leave it in the Hole, but I forgot with everything going on and left it at the normal spot.

I shoved back from the table and peeked underneath, but there was nothing there.

It was gone!

"But how is this possible?" I yelled at the table. "Unless... Trout was down here for a few minutes. Could he have taken—"

"WB9ZM0, this Blackstone Central calling you back."

I glared at the open bookshelf door, Dog now sitting up and staring at the ceiling.

Footsteps were coming our way.

And that meant I would have to unlock the door.

"WB9ZM0, are you reading me?"

The basement door handle was jiggled on the other end. "Open this pinche door!" a muffled yell boomed.

I was stuck. I had to turn off the radio and close the secret passageway, and I had to run up and open the door. But now, realizing that Trout probably had my bag with my records, including the recording where I admitted to shooting Polar Bear's son, Buster... I did the only thing I could think to do.

I ran.

CHAPTER 24

Ron

The drive back to OP's compound was silent, except for my deafening thoughts.

During previous trips, they tossed me into the back of one of their panel trucks to rattle around like so many loose parts. This time I was given the honor of the front passenger seat of the returning H2 Hummer. As if I were a VIP.

Anyone who didn't know OP might falsely assume this was a reward. I knew better. OP was about to test my loyalties, and it was because of some perceived or actual wrong.

This was made obvious from Trout's comment: "Mr. Ash will be coming with me to answer for what he's done." Of course, Trout enjoyed making comments like this one, just to fray our nerves. But I suspected there was some substance to his comment.

So during the long and quiet ride to OP's compound, I considered which one of our secrets they had discovered or what action one of us had taken, either of which could have been interpreted as a wrong committed against OP. I wouldn't have to guess for long, as OP would tell me face to face when we arrived at his compound. Immediately after, there was the short wait for his punishment. If lucky, I would be subjected to another beating from some of his psycho thugs. But if the committed "wrong" was perceived as more severe or if he ate a burrito that didn't sit well that day, I would be like so many others who got to feel the end of this sociopath's bloody scythe. It all depended on how the winds blew in this man's twisted mind.

The wait for this unknown end was maddening.

I got no help from my kidnappers.

I glanced again at Trout, who was driving and focusing all of his attention on keeping the Hummer's wheels from slipping off the icy road. I considered probing him for something more. Any piece of info which might reveal why OP was in such a hurry to retrieve me. But I knew Trout would say nothing more than he did when I had first asked: "OP is not happy and needs to see you now." He ignored all my other questions, only replying twice with, "OP will answer."

A quick glance at the other man in the back seat told me I'd get nothing from him. The Hummer's driver before this return trip had been sawing logs since we left. His face was a glitter of gold jewelry: a nose ring and gold studs that marked his lips, face and neck like stars in the night sky. He snored out breaths of air so putrid I had to cover my face. The .22 Winchester and .38 revolver they had taken from us rested on the seat next to him. These were oddities and further reasons for my building anxiety.

The taking of our two small caliber guns, and Trout's insistence at Matador staying at the house to learn how our growing operation worked felt very strange and ominous.

What could it be? Think Ronald, think!

My thoughts kept crashing back to Oak Tree and what he had said. Was it possible he had called to let OP know that I was hiding supplies? I had hoped not, based on the big man's comment that OP was "going to be angry," which would seem to indicate that Oak Tree didn't yet have time to radio in that he knew I was withholding supplies.

Nope, not that.

The other possibility, no matter how unlikely, was Joey's comment had finally made its way to OP.

Joey let it slip about Buster's golden gun, and that was unfortunate. But even as intelligent as Trout was, how could he connect all the dots to this one? And even if he had suspected this, without substantial proof, I doubted he would mention this to OP. If he did, OP might have Trout's hide for leading him to believe they had caught the killers of his miscreant son, Buster, all while he suspected the true killers were operating right under his nose.

Nope, I decided. That wasn't it, either.

Thinking this through logically somewhat arrested my anxiety over what was to come. And it helped me settle on a solution to the question. It had to be related to the problems OP and his thugs had been having with their vehicles, and what I specifically did to two of them.

Most survivors whose vehicles were in operation when the ash had started falling found their engines seizing up a month or so later. Turned out the highly abrasive ash clawed its way into all running engines, and then chewed up many of the engine's working parts. I had done my best to repair or replace the damaged parts in several of OP's engines, even installing additional filters to better protect them, though many were too far gone. Eventually, all those in operation during the ashfall would give out.

My instruction to OP was simple: The only thing he could do was park the vehicles he wanted to save and assume that those vehicles he drove would be driven into the ground fairly quickly. Only after the snow came and covered up the ash was it safe to bring the rest of his parked vehicles back into service. The pea-green Hummer we were in was one he had parked and had brought back into service because the other ash-clogged Humvees had been breaking down regularly.

There was another more permanent problem that would eventually do in all vehicles. It was one thing I had not told them about yet. However, it was the cornerstone to my plans for escape.

It all came down to the gas.

Standard fuel, after several months, would break down and eventually become unusable, often in as little as ninety days. It was even worse with the ethanol-enhanced gas found at our neighborhood gas stations. Diesel fuel lasted much longer, but not forever. And without treatment, they were not likely to get much more than a year out of it. Maybe two.

Before the world ended, when it felt like all supplies were infinite, most folks would have never suspected that there was a shelf life to everything, including the gas we put into our vehicles. OP would be no different in these assumptions. I was counting on this and his lack of engine knowledge.

In preparation, I had been experimenting with fuel additives, which could be used to boost the life of gasoline. I had a different purpose.

I only told his men that I was experimenting with additives to help improve their engines' performance, holding back the most important details. My larger plan required me to purposely kill two of his vehicles.

Had he discovered this?

If OP had uncovered my sabotage or somehow figured out my larger plan, he would certainly have been upset. Perhaps this was why I had been summoned.

Yep, I decided this had to be it. And if it was, I was done for.

This amped up my worry even more as we approached OP's gated compound entrance.

You'll figure a workaround like you always do, I reassured myself.

As we rolled into the compound, OP stood out immediately like some macabre welcoming party. He was rooted in place, like a hundred-year-old willow on the banks of the Guadalupe: unmovable by any force of man or nature. Everything and everyone moved around him.

His eyes were drilled into the ground in front of our incoming vehicle, his face a twisted scowl. And in his hand, he held his infamous scythe. Before him was a long splash-line of red in the dirty snow, telling me he had already fed his weapon in preparation for the next go-round. It was as if his scythe was a beast that had an unquenchable thirst for blood, and as its trainer, he chose on which of his unsuspecting victims he would release it.

Was I the beast's next victim?

As we came to a stop, OP's scowl lifted from the ground and found me through the windshield.

I knew then that all of my plans had just gone to hell.

CHAPTER 25

Nan

I was at a full-out panic by the time Matador went to retrieve Leticia.

Matador had demanded that we first show him all of the garden supplies, especially our storehouse of seeds, all of which we had kept in the garden. Then he demanded that I make him a meal, while he got his first "lesson"—that's what he called it—from Chloe.

At first, I was too busy fuming at the fact that I would have to pull from our meager rations to feed him to connect the dots. I kept hoping that they were going to bring us more supplies in a few days, to supplement what was barely enough to survive on ourselves. That's when the dots began connecting for me.

Ron had done something wrong and was being taken to OP "to answer for what he's done." Then there was the fact that Ron had been followed for some unknowable amount of time by one of OP's men, without any of us knowing it. Then Trout said that Matador was dispatched to us to learn what we knew so they could start a larger growing operation, even though Matador was known as one of their hit men and not a babysitter. Plus, his comment about verifying the supplies first then he'd... He never finished, but I got the sense that he was about to say "do his job"—like in as a hit man. Then, add that they had taken our two little popguns, which were all we had to defend ourselves against predators. It was as if they did not have any further use for us after today.

Could they be planning on killing us today?

But even if my estimations as to when were off, the ultimate problem was that I had caught a glimpse of Leticia's satchel being taken out of our house by Trout. I didn't realize it at the time. But now I knew. And though I didn't know half of what was in her recordings, I was sure there were many incriminating things about us. That meant that at some point in the near future, OP would learn what we were hiding. Of course, we didn't have the luxury of waiting until then. There was no chance we could live through this much longer than today. We had to do something now.

Their conversation in the greenhouse was pretty clear, as one of them left the door ajar. Matador had no intention of learning how to grow things. He was here to do a job. I was sure of it.

Then Matador's voice raised to his hollering a demand of where that "negra and her chuchó" went to. When Matador stormed out of the greenhouse to go check the bedrooms for Leticia, per Joey's suggestion, I sprang.

I dashed for the greenhouse to find Joey and Chloe whispering.

"We have to act fast," I said.

"What do you mean?" Joey asked.

"We need to capture Matador now. He's going to kill us all, no later than tomorrow morning when Trout returns."

Chloe's eyes grew wider than they already were.

There were more shouts for Leticia, and threats of death for her and dat chuchó rabioso, followed by a door being opened and slammed shut. Each door brought him closer to us and the one and only time we would be able to act.

"How could you know they're going to do this by tomorrow morning?" Joey asked, while putting his other hand on top of the one Chloe already clutched in a death grip.

"I overheard Trout say he was coming back tomorrow morning. Look, they don't need us anymore because they know how to grow things already—"

"I told you Matador was not interested in learning how we were doing what we were doing. He wasn't asking the right questions." Chloe offered, her voice rising several octaves as she gave her reasoning.

"But there are many other things too," I added. "Why take Ron and leave us with Matador, who is utterly useless, except acting badass and killing people? He certainly isn't their hope for growing food. I tell you, they don't need us anymore. And this may be the only time we have the numbers over one of theirs."

"Oh shit," Chloe hissed her acknowledgment of what I was suggesting.

Joey nodded once and then snapped his own head in one direction and then the next.

Matador banged on the basement door, only a few feet from the doorway into the greenhouse, but on an opposite wall. "Open up negra, or I will break the door down."

Joey looked more frantic, but then almost gave a smirk. He stuck his head in close to mine and whispered, "Closer" to Chloe.

"Okay," he said.

Matador banged louder than before. "This is your last chance. If I break down door, I kill the chuchó and hurt you." He banged again.

Joey whispered again, but loud enough that each of us could hear. "Let's hope Leticia is hiding in the Hole and can keep Dog muzzled. When Matador comes back here, and is sure that Leticia is actually hiding here, this is what we do..."

We listened to Joey's plan, keeping our heads close, while the report of Matador's rifle echoed loudly throughout the house.

There was a grunting sound, followed by the basement door being cracked open and a shower of splintered wood fragments rattling down the basement steps. Matador spewed indecipherable profanities in Spanish as he galloped downstairs.

While Matador stomped around in the basement, overturning shelving and screaming his frustration, we nodded and took our places.

CHAPTER 26

Ron

"Get up pendejo," Trout hollered and slapped the leg of the man sporting the facial jewelry in the back seat.

The man woke in an electric panic. Then he nodded, as if remembering where he was and his purpose here. But when he caught a glimpse of OP, his seizure-like mannerisms kicked back in.

"Flash," Trout said to the man, "you two stay in the vehicle." Trout didn't wait for acknowledgment, spun back in his seat and then exited.

Just then I saw something that shook me to my core.

With a gust of frosty wind rushing inside the open door, Trout reached back into the cab and grabbed a black satchel that at first looked like nothing special from the floorboard. I vaguely remembered him bringing it in with him from the house. It didn't click then. Now recognition struck me like a rattlesnake bite.

Leticia had a bag just like this. In fact, as Trout pulled the bag out and hoisted it over his shoulder, I knew it was Leticia's bag. And that meant we were sunk.

Leticia's bag was where she kept the voice recorder and SD cards I had given her. She often left us messages on various subjects because she had felt more at ease recording her voice rather than saying what she wanted to say to us in person. Other times, she asked us to record various anecdotes in our travails.

When she was done, she would pull the SD card and write one or two words about the recording on it. One of those cards had some information about Buster on it: I remembered seeing "Buster" written in her precise handwriting. When we first saw this card mixed in haphazardly with the other cards, I spoke to Leticia about being careful with this and any other cards; it could cause problems for us if she accidentally lost it or left it a place that OP's men could find it. I had asked her to leave her bag of trouble in the Hole. If this was in fact her bag, with her recorder and cards in it, we were so screwed.

I tried to consider when last I saw her bag. But I couldn't. I was too focused on my own unending to-do list.

Trout marched to within a few feet of OP and then stopped to say something I couldn't hear, because the windows were rolled up. He held up the bag and both he and OP looked back at me.

My heart skipped a terrifying number of beats.

OP said something else, and Trout signaled to Flash, his man behind me, to collect me. Trout then nodded at OP and walked away.

"Come on, man," insisted Flash. "Looks like the big boss wants to see you now." His voice quavered when he said 'big boss.'

I took a long breath and stepped out of the vehicle.

Approaching OP felt like walking to your own execution. And with each step toward this grim reaper, I felt more sure that my execution was going to happen right now. Trout very well might have understood Joey's comment, and now he had proof and he showed OP that he had the proof. And that was that.

Would the knife blade hurt? I wondered as I came within a few feet of Oso Polar.

I chose to stop just out of reach of OP and waited for him to speak. Everyone who knew OP knew that you never spoke first, unless you wanted to be assured of meeting the point of his knife. I may have been destined for this crazy man's knife, but I didn't want to hasten my inevitable demise.

His eyes dissected me from head to toe. Then he shook his head, like a father offering his disappointment to a child who had done something against his wishes, just before he was about to administer punishment. "I am not happy, my friend," he said in his deep voice that often reminded me of a psychotic James Earl Jones. OP turned and walked toward the back of the property, no doubt to the garage-side of the building.

"Follow me; we have much to discuss," he huffed.

Wait, it wasn't about Buster's killing. It was something else.

Before moving, I huffed out a giant breath of relief that I had been holding during OP's examination.

I might just survive this after all.

Then I shot a glance over to Trout, who was standing before one of the building's front entrances, sporting his own scowl at me. He too shook his head, showing his own dissatisfaction with me. Then he made a show of patting the black bag slung around his shoulder. Leticia's bag.

He was telling me that he had all he needed to catch us in our lies.

My death sentence was not commuted; it was merely postponed, and probably not for long.

Even without Leticia's recorded admission to Buster's murder, there was more than enough info on Leticia's recorded cards to fry each and every one of us: the fact that we had hidden food and supplies; that we had a radio, which was being used to reach out to other communities; and so many other details of our secret life which Leticia was sure to have spoken out about on her private recordings... Any one of them would be damning enough to end us.

But when Trout found and played the SD card titled "Buster," he was sure to have the proverbial smoking gun: Leticia's admission that she was the one who had shot and killed Buster with his own gun. He would then play it for OP, who would summarily execute each of us, starting with me.

Somehow, I had to get out of here and get back to the house and warn everyone.

The butt of Joey's .22 Winchester clanged against my solar plexus, sucking out some of my wind. "Boss said to follow him," commanded Flash. I had completely forgotten about this guy.

"Okay," I croaked and started marching in OP's direction.

Everywhere I looked, I saw no way out. We were going into the garage, I was guessing to talk about the vehicles. I had perhaps only a few minutes to do something before Trout uncovered our guilt. All the while we were in the middle of a compound, surrounded by armed men who would carry out anything OP requested, or face retribution in the form of ritual evisceration.

I rarely resorted to praying. But just then I did.

CHAPTER 27

Nan

The waiting and anticipation were the hardest parts of executing Joey's quickly conceived snare.

When I was a kid, my father showed me how to set up a rabbit snare. The mechanics of the whole thing instantly made sense to me: finding the spot where you knew the rabbit would go or offering bait to draw him in, creating a mechanism that would tangle up the rabbit, and then the snare itself that would tighten around its foot so that the rabbit was captured for good. Then, because I expressed doubt that the whole thing would work, Father made me wait uncountable hours for the rabbit to walk into our trap. Staying in one place without making a sound, while we watched and waited for that rabbit, and then the mental preparation for what would follow when we caught it, made me nauseous the whole time.

Our snare this time was for a much larger rabbit, and much more lethal. Each of us, individually, made up the crucial elements of our Matador snare trap. So we had no choice but to wait at our spots until our prey had come.

Finally, our rabbit, after banging around downstairs yelling profanities at an unfindable Leticia and Dog, was now coming our way.

Still, the anticipation of it all was eating at my insides. I'd have preferred to just stab the bastard and be done with it.

I glanced over at Chloe, our bait, and smiled at her. She did not smile back. I was the tripping mechanism of our rabbit snare, and I was long past ready. My hands couldn't have been any soggier than if we had been doing this in the rain. Joey, the other half our tripping mechanism, just stared at Chloe, his face a tangled web of worry lines, all for her.

Probably the Achilles heel of our trap was that each of us had to act as the snare when it was time. Would we be able to subdue this man together?

As if answering directly, Matador stomped up the basement staircase. Then he yelled, "If I find that little negra and her chuchó with you Chilo, one of you will die."

"Ready?" Joey whispered to me.

I nodded.

"Ready?" he asked Chloe.

Chloe nodded with her hands wrapped around her chest and then took her position. She grabbed a garden hoe and bent over to make like she was hoeing a track in the dirt, next to one we had just replanted with beans. This activity alone would have not drawn too much attention from our lecherous target. However, our bait had removed her shirt and was now virtually topless other than her bra, which barely held back her ample physique. And the way she leaned forward only ensured Matador would catch an eyeful of her very bountiful bosom when he approached our trap.

Matador was now up the stairs, about to enter the hall, only a few steps from the garden entrance.

"Where the hell are that negra and her ch—"

My hands clamped down on the rope, without pulling up the slack. It wasn't yet time. But almost.

My arms and legs tensed, ready to spring the millisecond I saw him...

That should be now.

We had thought he would walk all the way in before stopping, but he had obviously stopped before my tripwire and was maybe two or three steps from being visible. He may have frozen in his steps, but I heard his breathing.

Chloe looked up and acted surprised, holding her position. Then, even though I knew it killed her to do this, she forced a smile.

"Chica," he said, stepping forward. "What are you doing with—"

I pulled the rope up and held; Joey did the same on the other end.

Matador came into view at the same time his left foot caught my rope, sending him forward.

"What the..." he said before crashing face-first into the hard earth.

We sprang.

Joey was on him first, before Matador could attempt to right himself. Chloe dropped her hoe and leapt forward, and with both hands she pushed Matador's face back into the dirt, grinding his nose into the hard pack. I grabbed his left arm, yanked and sat with all my weight on the man's rear. Joey had jerked his right arm free and deftly slipped a rope around it and the left arm that I desperately held onto with both of my wet hands.

And like that it was over.

"¡Vete a la mierda! Estas muerta!" he spewed at us into the dirt. I won't even repeat the translation.

Joey stuck a rag into Matador's mouth, and I duct-taped this from cheek to cheek. Matador's eyes were wild with rage.

But Chloe, finally feeling empowered, said, "This is the last time your eyes will undress me, you prick." She scurried away and struggled to put on her long-sleeved shirt.

Matador appeared to shake as if he were getting electroshocked. But I realized that wasn't it: He was laughing. At us. His gesticulations grew, and seemed almost uncontrollable, as we picked him up from the ground and plopped him in a chair, tying each of his limbs to this.

His eyes were a flood of waterworks from his laughter. Then finally he settled down.

But none of us felt settled. We had just stirred up a huge hornet's nest and we weren't looking forward to who got stung to death.

None of us knew what to do next. Our plan came together much too quickly to figure in its aftereffects. But sometime later today, if not sooner, we would have to find some way to deal with Trout and probably more of OP's men.

We didn't have to wait long.

A squeak-tone announced someone was about to call on the radio.

We all spun on our heels, looking for it.

It was off to one side, where it must have landed after Matador's fall.

"Reporte, Matador," the radio blared.

That was one of OP's men calling Matador to report back.

CHAPTER 28

Ron

"Don't make me wait, Ronald," OP huffed from the side door entrance of what used to be Buster's garage. He disappeared into its dark interior.

I stopped at the doorway.

The vast garage had become a familiar space for me, but at that moment, I couldn't help but consider what was coming my way. So, to keep my nerves from overloading, I focused on the inside space.

The far end of the garage was almost invisible in the low light cast from one open rear garage door. It was used for storage, just as Buster had done, though now, it was mostly a place where they stored everything they didn't know what to do with, but they still thought retained value. Their food storage had been relocated to someplace else I didn't know, no doubt with better protection from the many kleptomaniacs who paraded through this place. So most of what occupied the garage was floor-to-ceiling piles of junk. A chaos of junk, which kept growing and encroaching into the space where the few vehicles were parked at this end.

The apocalypse meant that OP's vehicles constantly needed service. And I must have been the only mechanic around, as I was constantly being brought here to work on them. Vehicles that needed fixing were repaired here. Sometimes I could convince OP that I needed to work on parts of an engine in my basement workshop. Those parts were then reinstalled, and the vehicles were turned around and put back into service or stored at another location. With only two exceptions, the few vehicles inside the garage were there temporarily, to either pull out parts or for service.

It was the two exceptions that concerned me.

And the fact that I was being called inside here, instead of his office, is what set me on edge. The day Joey and I first entered this garage flooded back.

That was when we killed Buster's men and then Leticia killed Buster with his own golden gun. The same golden gun that he used to kill Leticia's parents.

"Keep moving, pendejo," Flash demanded from behind, "unless you want to die here." Once again, he ratcheted the butt of the Winchester against my already sore shoulder, where he practically broke it the first time.

Forward I went, imagining the worst of what awaited me inside, unable to see where I was going.

"Come here, Ronald," OP beckoned, his booming voice seemingly coming from different points in the garage all at once, making this place even more ominous.

The low light provided one welcome mental diversion: I had to work at avoiding running into anything sharp sticking out of the continually growing clutter of tools and materials that were added to the shop part of the garage.

Focus on controlling your breathing, I told myself. But I was failing miserably at this. Why were none of the lights on?

It took my eyes an unbearable amount of time to adjust. Then I saw OP standing in front of one of his newer black Humvees. I knew this particular Humvee quite well. On its hood was an strange object, which didn't belong but I couldn't quite make out.

When the object resolved itself, I had to suck down my reaction and pretend that it was nothing.

It was everything.

It was Buster's golden gun, with its barrel pointed at me. I would have recognized it anywhere. And the meaning of this display was obvious: OP knew the truth and he was confronting me with it. Right now.

"Do you know why you are here now?" OP asked, his voice robotic.

I couldn't take my eyes off the gun when I knew I should have ignored it and stared directly at OP instead.

Flash clanked the Winchester against my back again to remind me that our superior had asked me a direct question.

"Stand down," OP hissed at Flash, who shuffled a foot or two away from me. "Your answer?" he asked. One of his bushy white brows furrowed.

"No," I said succinctly, opting to give away as little as possible. If I said anything more, my gut-crushing fear would show. If it wasn't already.

"Do you want to tell me why you think we are here?" OP asked. His voice had grown gruffer with each question he asked.

"I suspect,"—I took a gulp of air—"it has something to do with that Humvee and the gun on its hood."

"Damn, you are smart for a white boy, aren't you?" he barked.

I pushed him too far. "I didn't mean anything by this." I took in another shuddering gulp of air. "I just really don't know." I stated this with as much sincerity as I could muster. My whole life, I generally sucked at lying. Liz could always catch me during those rare times I held something back from her. But lying had become easier for me since she left me. I lied daily to my friends to protect me and them from the truth. At that moment, I swore that if I could get out of this one, I would come completely clean with my friends. I'd tell them everything.

"Okay, let's try this," OP said. He reached up and snatched the golden cannon from the hood. With his other hand, he pointed to the windshield.

There was movement behind it. Someone was in the driver's seat, and I had not noticed him, until now.

The Humvee's engine turned over and ran for a few seconds. But then it sputtered, a piston or two not firing right. And then it stopped, belching out black smoke from the exhaust. It was one of the two vehicles I had purposely killed.

OP lifted the gun and pointed its barrel at my face. The bore hole equaled the diameter of his beefy forefinger. "I'll ask you this just once. What did you do to my engine?"

Trout

The contents of the negra's bag were spilled out in a heap on top of my desk. It was one yellow digital recorder, a couple of notebooks, including a log book, and maybe a hundred memory cards. Each memory card had carefully written words on it. I sifted through the pile, unsure of what I was looking for, but stopped the moment I saw one titled "Buster."

I knew that you gringos had something to do with Buster's murder; I just couldn't prove it.

We had tracked down the group of survivalists and they admitted to the theft of Buster's supplies and killing him and his men. But that was only after torturing them. All I can say is that I too would have admitted to Buster's murder, if I was on the receiving end of our torture. But other details did not add up as well. Yet OP told us all "good job" and that was all. We were done with Buster.

But then we found your group and that got me wondering if we tortured the wrong people after all. This felt right when Chavo here said something about a golden gun. Because you don't see those often. And now I was sure I had proof.

I shoved the "Buster" card into the recorder and pressed play. The little girl began speaking. "I must explain why I did what I d—"

Someone pounded on my door and so I had to stop the playback.

"Señor Silas," tentatively announced a juvenile voice behind the door, "my dad say he need to talk at you about Matador."

As much as I wanted to spend more time listening to the recordings, OP had asked me to go get the Twins and now OP's buffoon cousin, Matador needed something. Besides, I thought, whether or not I had proof that one of them was guilty wouldn't matter by tomorrow morning.

Items left unattended on my desk had the habit of running off on their own. So I shoveled everything back into the bag and slung it around my shoulder.

"What's the problem?" I asked and opened the door.

"He not answering the radio," said Pequeño Miguel, the son of one of OP's men. PM ran errands for us around the compound.

"Thank you, PM," I said. "Your English is getting better."

"Thank you, Señor Silas," he said with a big smile.

"Now go to the garage," I told him. "OP will need help cleaning up the bloody remains of Mr. Ash."

CHAPTER 29

Nan

"Reporte Matador," the voice called out. The three of us just stared at each other.

"I don't think we should answer them," Chloe said.

"But if we don't answer, they'll send everybody here," I said.

"True, Matador must answer," Joey said, and then surprised both of us by ripping Matador's duct tape to one side and pulling out his gag.

"We can't let him answer," I tried to state, but was interrupted by Matador.

"You are all dead," he spewed in his gravelly voice. "Do you think I'm going to answer to save your asses? Of course not."

Joey smiled, his eyes glued to Matador's mouth. He held the radio out, as if he were certainly planning on getting Matador to talk on our behalf.

"Matador, this is Trout. Report," the radio bellowed.

"That is my boss, Chavo. If I don't report in, he will send OP's army. You will all die, but not before he lets me have my fun with you." He turned his head and shoulders so that he was facing Chloe. "Especially y—"

Joey shoved the gag back into his mouth, and then reapplied the tape. He slapped Matador's face and in a voice which sounded exactly as if Matador were speaking, he said, "Thanks, Chavo."

Chloe and I did a double take.

Joey clicked the transmit button.

"Hey boss," he said, not only correctly mimicking Matador's tone, but his swagger. "Sorry, I was having my fun with that pretty chica."

"You have not killed them yet?" Trout asked.

Chloe gaped at Joey, who momentarily flashed anger, but then let it pass.

"No, not yet," he answered, a little more like Joey then.

"Good. Are they tied up?" Trout asked.

"Yes, of course." Joey answered, with the Matador swagger back in his voice.

"Good. Did they show you where all their garden supplies are?"

"Yes. What next?"

"Don't hurt them yet. Wait for me. I'm coming there later. I may have them confess to something before you do anything. Then you can do whatever you want with them, including all of the women."

Joey glared at Matador who, even with his mouth covered in tape, bore a smile and began giggling, though it sounded like he was choking. Joey took a step closer and clobbered him with a right fist to the man's cheek. He clicked the transmit button with his left. "Okay, boss. I'll wait for you. I have them all secured in their garden."

"Trout out."

Joey let his head fall and he marched over to the small worktable we all used and let the radio drop on top of it, knocking several items off.

I understood what he was feeling, and I articulated it. "Well, that took us out of the frying pan and shoved us right into the fire."

"But why?" Chloe asked. "We've got one and soon we'll have the other, when that Trout asshole comes here."

"Okay, I'll bite." Joey tossed her a sarcastic glance. "How do we do that?"

“Simple,” she said. "Same as Matador." She flashed a sly grin. "Only we'll use Matador's gun when Trout comes into the garden, and we take Trout by surprise. He won't be expecting it. He's expecting us to be tied up, not the other way around."

Joey's hands were now planted on his hips. "Then what, you know, after you execute this precise military operation to perfection?"

His words dripped sarcasm, and so I was staying out of this one. Not because I wanted to avoid getting in the middle of a lover's spat, but as much as I thought Joey and I were on the same page, I was hopeful that Chloe might prompt Joey to come up with a way out of this. Because I had nothing.

She looked like an injured bird. "Well..." Chloe's eyes went from Joey to me and back, eyelashes fluttering. "Once we have those two, we could call OP and tell him we want to trade for Ron." She sounded less than sure.

"Seriously? That's your great plan?" Joey huffed.

"What? It might work," Chloe shrugged.

She wasn't getting it and Joey wasn't helping. "Aren't you forgetting something big?" I asked.

"What?" Chloe asked without looking up.

"They were planning on killing us anyway. Even if we could exchange Ron for OP's men, what makes you think that OP won't just kill us all after this?"

She looked up, eyelids flapping furiously like butterflies in a windstorm. Her mouth pursed. "I hadn't figured that one out yet."

Joey pounded the table with a balled fist. "Okay, all I've got is that we wait for Trout. Then we capture him"— he looked at Chloe—"similar to the way Chloe suggested. Then maybe we can force either Trout or Matador to tell us what happened to Ron and how to find him. Then I'll sneak into the compound and free Ron."

Before either of us could respond to Joey's crazy idea, Matador now sounded like he was gagging on something. But quickly, we all knew it was just him laughing at us again.

I didn't care to hear what he had to say, but Joey yanked off his gag again. "Okay what's so damned funny?"

"Your man Ron is already dead. Trout say OP was going to kill him after he finds out what Ron did to his engines. He's already been shot by now."

CHAPTER 30

Ron

This time I don't hesitate to answer. "I can explain. This is a larger problem that I didn't expect to hit for a while. But I have a plan to solve it." My words tumble out in one breath. "It's not just you; this also is going to happen to every vehicle in the world. Soon."

OP's brows furrowed even further and he clicked back the gun's hammer to make it clear that he was not kidding around. "So, you plan on destroying everyone's engines, not just mine?"

"Mmm-mmm," Flash hummed in agreement from behind me.

"What? No!" I said; one of my palms rose up in an unconscious effort to shield myself—as if that would work—and plead for more time to explain. "No, this happened because your gasoline is going bad. So I've been testing a fix on some of your vehicles, including this one. Obviously, this specific fix didn't work."

"That's bullshit," snarled Flash. His feet shuffled closer and I could feel his fetid breath on the back of my neck. "Tell da truth," he bellowed.

"I am. All gasoline has a shelf life of only a few months to as long as maybe one year, depending on where it comes from. Gas is a highly refined substance with very complex molecular bonds which naturally break down to an unusable state. That is, unless you treat the gas. This is happening right now."

Flash shoved me. "No, that ain't right. You did thi—"

Boom! thundered the golden cannon.

A thud sounded behind me and I turned to see Flash lying in a lifeless heap, his facial jewelry, as well as most of his face, gone. I spun back to OP. His gun was now pointing down. He was shaking his head. "Flash came to me and said that he saw you pouring some liquid into my gas tank, because he said you wanted to damage my vehicles. I didn't believe him, but he insisted that you were up to no good. I just needed to hear you to know the truth. I see no lies on you."

He tossed the gun back onto the hood with a loud clunk and approached me.

He put his arm around my shoulder. "I have always hated that gun. But my useless boy insisted on it to make up for his being a small man. He thought it made him look bigger, more macho."

With his free hand, OP unsheathed his scythe. "I prefer a more intimate tool, to cut to the heart of the matter."

OP guided me toward the storage side of the garage, which also exited into the motel and the offices. "So why don't you tell me all about your plan to fix all of this," he said accenting each syllable with his scythe like a conductor uses a baton to guide his orchestra's musical movements.

The meaning of this was unmistakable. I had been given a reprieve. For now. But that was subject to my not damaging any more of his vehicles and providing him a solution for the problem that I had identified. And he wanted it now.

"Okay. As I mentioned, your and everyone else's fuel is breaking down and very soon will be completely useless. Unless you find a way to get the refineries back up and running..." This was a huge fib on my part. His fuel was certainly going to break down, just not anywhere as quickly as I had led on.

We walked past the other truck I had destroyed while testing my newest formula. I focused on him and not the truck.

"Well, the solution is simple. A gas additive. I tried to make my own, which was what I was testing." I nodded at the truck so that he wouldn't see the lie. "But I rummaged through my records and found that there was a place, just outside of town, that had the base additive you will want to add to each of your vehicles and to your gas supply. And if you do this, your fuel should last for years."

OP stopped us, long before reaching the back exit into the motel and offices. "What if we needed to protect a very large supply of fuel—would you have enough of this... additive?"

"How large?" I asked.

"Over fifty thousand."

"Gallons?"

"Yes. We took over several big tanks of gasoline and diesel fuel. You see, we have many plans to expand our operations into other states now. And to do this, we will need fuel. As you mentioned, this is more important now because of this fuel breakdown everyone but us will be experiencing." He smiled at his last statement.

I couldn't believe he was taking the bait—hook, line and sinker. "Yes, I think there's more than enough additive to take care of all your gas supply."

OP was facing me now, and at some point when I was speaking, he had re-sheathed his scythe. "That is good news, Mr. Ronald." He said my name this way when he was pleased. "Please tell me where I can get this additive and I'll send my men there."

Just then it occurred to me how I could get away. Or at least, how I could give myself a chance to do so.

"Sir, it's actually hidden in a warehouse area I don't think you know about yet. If you can give me one of your H1 Humvees and one of your men, we can get it all by tonight."

OP thought for just a moment, before answering. "I'll give you two of my best men." He whistled and the garage door entrance popped open. One of OP's older guards hurried out, his hands on a weapon slung across his chest. "Si, El Jefe." He had been waiting for OP's orders.

OP spat rapid-fire Spanish at the guard, who nodded, spun on his heals and darted back through the doorway to carry out his orders.

OP turned us around and ushered me back to the exit door in which we had entered. "Okay, Mr. Ronald Ash." When he used my full name, he had a serious point to make. "You will have two Humvees and two men to help. You wait out front and they will get you. I am trusting you to do as you say." He stopped me once again and spun me around so I was facing him so he could glare his dark eyes at mine. "But listen to my warning. If you do anything but what you say, I will have my men execute your pretty lady friends, the chavo and your dog. Do we understand each other?"

OP thus revealed the reason for Matador being stationed at our house. The man would carry out execution orders as soon as he was told. And when either Trout listened to the proof that Leticia murdered OP's son, or I attempted escape—which I had to do—OP would be making that call.

"You couldn't be more clear, sir."

CHAPTER 31

Leticia

"I need to tell you something," I said to the three of them when we were alone in the basement.

Dog was by my side, giving me the strength and support I needed for my confession.

"I'm worried about two things," I said, looking at the floor.

Joey had been pacing the room, occupied with his own thoughts, while Nan and Chloe were arguing about the fish man.

The women stopped and looked at me with their kind eyes, just like my mother used to do when I had hurt myself.

"First, I messed up, and I am afraid that this will mean that the Polar Bear will come after me, and probably all of you."

Joey had stopped pacing. Nan and Chloe's expressions changed to those of concern.

"What could you have possibly done to make you think the cartel boss is going to come after you? Or us?" Nan asked.

"You know that voice recorder that Ronald gave me?"

They nodded their heads. Nan glanced at the shelf where I often kept the bag when I wasn't wearing it around me.

"Well, that fish man has it."

"That's all right, sweetie. We'll get you a new recorder," Joey said, but he didn't have those kind eyes like the others.

"So why is that a problem, Leticia?" Nan asked. She looked ready to jump out of her skin. Though I never understood how someone could do that in real life.

"Well, you know how I record things on the voice recorder using those little SD memory cards?"

"Yes, of course," Chloe said. "You left all of those wonderful messages for us all the time, along with some notes... back when you didn't speak much."

"And you titled each card to tell us what they were about," Joey added. "But I don't see how that..." He looked at me like he understood what I was thinking, even though I hadn't said anything yet.

"Well, one of them was named 'Buster' and on it, I talked about how my parents were killed and..." I looked up at each of them and based on their tight faces, they all seemed to understand what I was about to say. "Well, I also admitted to killing Buster with his gold gun."

"Oh shit!" Nan said, and then under her breath, "We are so screwed."

"Honey," Joey appeared to be ignoring Nan, "what exactly happened to your bag and the card with 'Buster' written on it?"

"Trout stole it," Nan answered. "I saw him walk out the door with it."

"And you didn't say anything?" Joey asked.

"We haven't exactly had the time," Nan responded.

"Leticia," Chloe called out. Her voice was a distant tremble, even though she was leaning into me. Her eyes drilled into mine. "You said there were two things you wanted to discuss with us. Wa-what was the other?"

Joey was about to ask something, but he clammed up to hear my next confession. Though now, after admitting to my big error, I didn't want to admit to anything more.

"Go ahead, honey," Nan insisted. She was wearing her caring eyes again.

"Okay, but it seems silly now with everything that's going on."

"Please tell us," Joey said, looking put out by my hesitation.

"Well, it's about Ronald... I think..." I couldn't help it. I started to cry like a baby. I hadn't cried much, as far as I could remember. I didn't even cry when my parents were killed, or after. I cried a little after recording my "Buster" confession. But that was it.

I sobbed. And to their credit, all three put their arms around me. And when I was done, I noticed none of them had dry eyes either.

"It's okay, Leticia," Joey said, no longer looking annoyed with me. "Go ahead and tell us what you have to about Ron."

I took a breath and spat it out. "I think Ronald is going to leave us. I followed him out of his secret passageway, and—"

"What secret passageway?" Joey asked.

"Let her continue. You can interrogate her later," Chloe said.

"Well, I followed him to this building and there I saw that he had one vehicle that he was filling up with supplies."

I took a breath and saw that the adults were looking at each other like they were aware of all of this but keeping it from me. This hurt too.

"But the thing is, there was only room for one person in the driver's seat and Dog. There wasn't room for anyone else. Just him and Dog, and all those supplies. So, you see, even if you're able to free Ronald somehow, he will be leaving us."

"Best not to worry about that right now," Joey said, not just to me, but to the adults too. "We have to plan on how we're going to first get the fish man"—he said this to me—"and then we'll get Ron. Then we will figure out where we are all going, together. Okay?"

We all nodded. Then Joey told us his plan for freeing Ronald.

CHAPTER 32

Ron

It was impossible.

Breaking in so that they could grab the additive was the easy part. But escaping this place without getting shot was going to be unimaginably difficult.

Somehow, I had to try.

I was considering the how part when we pulled up to the warehouse. There were no tracks there, presumably since the ones I had made a month earlier. That was when I first concocted this whole getaway scheme and began its execution.

At that time, it was a really simple plan. The bulk additive was located in five-gallon plastic drums, stored on four tiers of shelving inside a supply warehouse, only minutes from town. I had previously confirmed the supply and took a few drums for myself. Then all I had to do is spike each of the drums with my concoction. The magic would happen after I was gone. When OP or his men used the spiked additive in their vehicles, it would appear to at first help the vehicle run better. Then my chemical cocktail would start to gum up the engine and make it unusable. That was, without a complete overhaul. OP's two dead vehicles were the results of my tests.

Once I identified the source, the hardest part was figuring out how to deliver the chemical cocktail into the additive, while not breaking each drum's seal. A horse syringe from an ignored vet clinic provided my solution.

On the side of the barrel, by the stamps, I could plunge in the syringe and deliver the spoiling agent. When I withdrew it, I simply used a dab of clear epoxy to seal it. Unless someone closely inspected each drum, they'd never know the drums had been tampered with.

The big problem now was the timing. I thought I had a couple more days, but then OP's twins changed everything.

Unfortunately, I had only enough time to spike the first tier of drums. There were three other shelves above these, each packed with similar drums. So at most, just 25% of the drums were spiked. There was clearly no time to get around this. Somehow, I had to convince OP's men that we should take only the first tier of barrels. But with Trout about to reveal Buster's real killer, if he hadn't already, there was no way I'd have any time to return and spike the remainder. The simple plan just got indescribably complex.

Somehow, I needed to get one vehicle loaded up with only the first tier of spiked drums, and then figure out a way to damage the remaining supply, such that it wouldn't make OP suspicious so that he would use the spiked additive. Then, by some miracle, I needed to get away. And I needed to do this very quickly.

How in the hell are you going to do all that, Ronald? I asked myself.

The prospect of just escaping seemed almost impossible now that OP had me shadowed by the two well-armed, mute twins who looked like they could spit nails.

The mute part was a guess since I had not heard either of them speak a word. But twins was a definite: they looked like clones of each other, right down to their bald heads and deeply tanned skin. Plus, they were called the Twins. Though it wasn't the fact that these siblings shared blood that made my task near impossible.

I had met some pretty scary men in the last few years, especially because of Buster's love of boats. Evidently, he appreciated my work so much that the word in scary-guy circles got around. Still, these two got the scary-guy prize, hands down.

Perhaps that was OP's goal: frighten me into compliance. It worked.

Each twin drove one of OP's H1 Humvees to get us here. I was in the lead vehicle. The other was parked behind us in the warehouse parking lot.

As we sat there, I glanced at the bald driver for some sort of acknowledgment of what he wanted us to do next. He just stared into his rear-view mirror at his brother, inside the other Humvee behind us.

"Do you want to go inside now?" I asked.

The man ignored me, turning his attention to his radio unit when it chirped and then sang out one long, indecipherable sentence in Spanish.

The mute twin held the radio in his hand, and glared at it, as if he were unsure what to do next. Once again, he sought help from his rear-view mirror.

The radio chirped again, followed by a "Si" in a voice deeper than OP's.

"Perhaps we should go ask your brother?" I asked, not trying to hide my sarcasm.

Still, he didn't answer. But when I moved to open my door, his response was instantaneous. In one quick blur, the mute twin snatched his silver handled pistol from his cross-draw holster, and pointed it at my head.

My reply was equally quick: Both my hands shot up into the air.

On the mute's driver's side window, there was movement. It was his brother, standing outside and staring in.

I wondered if his brother spoke the simple "Si" a moment ago, or if that was someone else.

My mute twin opened the door and stepped out. Each of them silently glared at the other, as if they were communicating via ESP. My mute nodded to his brother, as if getting his unspoken marching orders from his sibling. He then marched around to my side, where he opened my door and motioned with his already drawn silver pistol for me to exit. He pushed us at a diagonal to our Humvee, toward the warehouse and to his brother, on the other side.

With both Humvees' head lamps on, I got a good view of both men now. They were virtually identical. Each man was built like an NFL fullback; each sported a head as bald as a baby's bottom; and each had a face completely vacant of all humanity. They were like robots, who did what OP, their programmer, demanded.

I felt an immense sense of dread at that moment.

I wondered if I could not break free from these two, would they still be given an order to kill me? The dread was in knowing that these two probably never failed their orders.

CHAPTER 33

Nan

We captured Trout without a shot.

Once again, Joey came up with another elaborate snare to nab him and his driver, if one showed up. But we didn't really need it.

We had left the front door unlocked and the front door shutter up, just like we would if we were expecting a next-door neighbor to come over for dinner. But we had no idea when Trout would arrive. Certainly not as early as he did. Less than half an hour after we had decided on a plan, he sashayed in like he owned the place, hollering, "Matador, where are you?"

Joey was in the kitchen with his back to the front door. I was pouring him a cup of tea. Upon hearing Trout's voice, Joey spun around, greeting him with Matador's gun and said in his Matador voice, "He's in the garden."

Realization hit Trout immediately. He nodded and said, "Smart, Chavo. I was speaking to you and not Matador on the radio today, wasn't I?"

Joey just smiled.

Trout gave up his pistol, radio and more importantly, Leticia's bag. Leticia was on it like a buzzard on fresh roadkill.

We lashed up Trout's arms and legs to a chair and parked him next to Matador in the garden.

After getting worked up at Trout's arrival, Dog now slept on his favorite pile of dirt, at the far end of the garden. He knew, and so did our captives, he was only a couple of strides away.

Once Trout was secured, Leticia brought out a chair and suggested we record his interrogation.

"Why, for God's sake?" I asked. It seemed so frivolous. In fact, if I had been holding Matador's gun rather than Joey, I might have put a bullet into each of them.

"Because I want it," Leticia said while rummaging through her bag, grumbling about how everything was out of order. She grabbed an SD card with a smile, pulled out the one already in the recorder, and slipped the new one in its place. She tossed the discarded SD—without looking at it—

in her bag, and then paused to look at me with her sweet but always serious face. "For the same reason I have been having you and Ronald record what you experienced each week. I want to write our story, after we find our ultimate home." She returned her gaze to the recorder and then Trout, finally clicking the recorder's red button.

"This is the Interrogation of Silas "Trout" Guzman, 176 Days after The World Event." She unclicked the record button.

I gave Leticia a double-take. Her words continued to surprise me, as one who barely spoke when she first came to us, to now, when she proved to be impressively articulate for a thirteen-year-old. And the fact that she thought so highly of our chances of a future, after everything that had happened to us, warmed my heart. Then to have the foresight to want to record this interrogation for a future book filled me with hope that I had such difficulty finding on my own these days. But the greatest surprise about her statement was that she had kept track of the exact number of days that had passed since what I assumed was the day the first volcano erupted. This floored me. This girl had the composure of someone so much wiser than her years. Wiser than all of us.

"Maybe," Leticia looked at Joey, knowing he wanted to run the interrogation, "after you get what you want, I'd like you to ask him what led his group to finding us—you know, after they first rolled into town?" She then made a show of clicking the record button and placing the recorder in her lap.

Joey shrugged and after a moment nodded to Leticia. "Okay, sure honey. We might as well start there." Turning to Trout, he said, "Trout, how the hell did you find us?"

Trout went on to explain how when OP and his men arrived to find Buster murdered, Trout was instrumental in setting up a dragnet for Buster's killers.

He also told us about how crazed OP was about finding his son's killer and how he would carve out a hole in his son's desk, acting out as if he were stabbing the killer himself.

As he described this part, he glanced back at us for our reactions.

Finally, he described how they had narrowed their search down to one group, and they stormed the house of that group. Thankfully, it ended up being an unrelated survivalist group instead of us.

"But I always knew it had to be one of you," he said, while flashing his permanently fixed smile. It was obvious he enjoyed this whole exercise. I was tiring of it, and evidently, so was Joey.

"Cut the crap, Trout. Tell us why you were planning on having your henchman here"—he nodded toward Matador—"kill us?"

Trout's face twisted for a moment as if he were in pain, then the smile came back. "Friends, that was all a misunderstanding. We were not—"

"Misunderstanding?" I cut in, now more angry than shocked, as we were when we first heard this on the radio. "You asked Matador—which was actually Joey—quote, you have not killed them yet? End quote... That's not a misunderstanding. That's a plan."

Trout readjusted in his chair, attempting to move his smile even farther up his face. "Well, that has all changed."

"What's changed?" Joey asked.

Trout didn't hesitate, obviously feeling the pressure of our questioning. "When I found the little girl's bag with the tapes and—"

"They're recorded SD cards; not magnetic tapes," instructed Leticia. Her head was now turned up at him, while she sat in a chair a few feet away, cradling the recorder.

Trout let a smirk crawl back up his face—and I did too —"Okay, cards... Anyway, when I saw all of them, I knew that was where I would find proof that you were all guilty of many things... including killing Buster." He glanced more slowly at each of us, still probing for a reaction. His gaze stopped on Leticia, who was looking away and tapping a foot as she often did when she got nervous. "So I was anxious to get to my office and listen to them..."

Trout then went on to explain how he ran out of time before he could listen to any of the cards because he had to attend to the radio, which was when Joey pretended to be Matador.

"So you listened to the cards and that is what changed?" Joey asked, showing his frustration.

I felt frustrated too. It was like he was purposely wasting our time.

"Well, no. And because there were so many cards, I realized that I would never have enough time to listen to all of them."

"So why are you here now?" I asked in my I-am-pissed-off voice.

"Because I felt pressure to get to the bottom of this, before Mr. Ash finished his current mission with the Twins, winning him even more favor with the boss."

Joey and I both shot glances at each other, but for different reasons.

"What current mission?" I asked.

Joey started pacing the room.

"Just something he's pretending to do for OP," Trout said. "But I suspect Mr. Ash is up to something."

"So, what did you hope to accomplish by coming here now?" Joey asked, while still pacing.

"I thought that, while I still had time, I could speed this up by... what is it you Americans say... appealing to your sense of self-preservation. I would get one of you to admit to—"

Chloe had been quietly standing back in the corner, behind the workbench, when she became animated and yelled, "You're talking torture; you were going to torture one of us." She glanced at Leticia. "Like Leticia—you'd get one of us to say what you wanted."

"I would never torture a child," Trout said, acting hurt at the accusation.

"Maybe not you." Joey halted his pacing to lean into Trout. "But you'd have no problem using your henchman here." He nodded toward Matador.

Matador's head had been snapping from side to side, following each of us as we spoke, as if he were watching a doubles tennis match. Still, his face was emotionless. Maybe he was even bored.

Trout shrugged his shoulders. "Anyway, that does not matter now. While coming down here, I found the tape—I mean card—labeled 'Buster' and played it." He glared at Leticia. "On it, this one admits to killing OP's son."

We couldn't help it; except for Leticia, who was glaring holes in her tapping foot, we gaped at each other before returning our attention to Trout. He had us dead to rights.

"Too bad you didn't have time to tell Mr. Bear?" Joey said, inflecting Bear as if it were a question.

"Oh, I told him, just before I walked in here."

"We should just kill both of them and leave. He was going to have us killed." I said this in a monotone voice, as if it was normal thing to kill two people. But the thing was... I meant it.

"Like I said, that is not necessary," Trout said, the smirk long gone from his face. "Polar Bear changed his mind and does not want to kill everyone. He just wants to talk to her... the little girl."

"I have a name," Leticia yelped. A scowl hung on her face for a long moment. "It's Leticia."

"As I was saying. I was going to grab the little—I mean Leticia," Trout cast a quick glance to her and then gave Joey his full attention, even though I was the one who just talked about killing him. "Then I was going to try and convince OP that the rest of your people needed to live." He forced another smile.

This set me off. I snapped my fingers and demanded his attention. "Excuse me. Why would you care whether we lived or not, other than because we have a weapon pointed at your fish-like head?"

"Simple. My boss killed two people because of his anger, and we needed both to survive. One drove our big trucks, and I understand that Chavo here"—He motioned with his shoulder at Joey— "can do this too. And one guy, with a lot of experience, was supposed to head our growing operations. But after OP summarily executed him, the job was going to go to this buffoon." Trout motioned at Matador, whose face turned from boredom to surprise and then to anger in a millisecond. "Anyway, the rest of you know how to grow things and could manage our operations in town. And it's obvious that Mr. Ash is OP's golden boy. He can do no wrong."

"Thought you said you were racing to get the goods on Ron and break OP's trust in him," I interrupted.

Trout threw out a momentary scowl and then corrected it back to a smile, "True-true. You caught me, Chilo. But after finding the guilty party, I knew I no longer needed to race."

Trout's radio blared; someone rattling off something in Spanish.

I glared at Trout when Señor Ash was mentioned. "A lot of that didn't make sense," I said. "Translate what he said about Señor Ash."

Trout smiled. This time it was real. He took a breath like he had all the time in the world and then said, "One of my people is trying to tell J and J—we also call them the Twins—after they are finished, to bring Mr. Ash back to this house. There is... Well, that's it."

"Who are the Twins?" Joey asked.

I didn't want to hear the answer, but I knew we needed to, even though it felt like we were wasting our time here with Trout.

"They're killers from Mexico," Trout announced. "OP uses them when he needs an important job done. We call them the Twins because they are twin brothers who look exactly alike. They are both named Juan and they are the best killers in the business. I've never heard them talk. For this reason and another, they creep me out."

"Why would they creep you out?" Joey asked.

"If you see the Twins show up and they are paying any attention to you, it is because you are dead already and you just do not know it. And I have heard they have never failed to kill their target. They would rather suffer unbelievable pain and die than fail their mission."

I couldn't help it. I had to ask. "So... why are they with Ron? He's not a... target, is he?"

"I do not know. It sounds like they are doing some sort of supply pick up with Mr. Ash. So maybe OP is having them do some sort of babysitting because he is either afraid Mr. Ash might escape, or because OP wants to protect Mr. Ash from someone else. But I do know that OP trusts the Twins above everyone, even me, to do their job."

Joey asked the question that occurred to me as well. "Have you heard of the Twins doing any sort of babysitting or protection operation before—you know, besides killing?"

"No."

CHAPTER 34

Ron

My mute's brother motioned with his own matching sterling silver pistol, and said "Vamos!" This of course answered the question about whether either of them could speak.

"You Mexican cartel members sure like your shiny guns," I said, testing to see if they understood anything coming out of my mouth. I was also trying to buy time to figure out what I could do next to increase my chances of escape, if anything.

They both just glared at me with their lifeless eyes.

I marched ahead of them. My long shadow from both Humvees' headlights marked a path toward the warehouse's side entrance, shrinking and becoming more pronounced with each footstep. The twins didn't appear to have shadows and I almost turned to see if they were still there. But like two ghosts emerging from nothing, their dark shadows stalked their way toward me. It was as if they preferred to travel in some ethereal form, hugging the darkness, until they chose to materialize so they could conclude their business.

At the door, it struck me that I didn't have the key. I had not planned on going to this warehouse today and so I had left the key hidden in my secret room. While I was trying to think of how to tell these two bald specters, who for all I knew didn't speak any English, about this problem, my mute whipped out his silver pistol and shot two .45 slugs into the lock. Then, in one fluid movement, he kicked the door open. He stepped back, re-holstered his weapon and waited for me to enter first.

I know I stood in front of the doorway for several long moments, completely stunned. My remaining nerve endings were finally unraveling then, and I felt a consuming desperation take hold. How was I, a boat mechanic, going to get away from these two demons, who seemed all but unstoppable?

Focus, Ronald, I told myself, and stepped into the dark warehouse.

Although the headlights provided enough light to discern the walkway from the shelves and aisles, I clicked on the flashlight always attached to my belt and marched forward. A thought occurred to me: Maybe these two could see nocturnally... A wave of shivers took over. My pace increased, as I knew to head toward the middle of the warehouse where the high-test fuel and fuel additives were stored.

I didn't even dare to look back and check if the twins of death were behind me. Their footsteps were silent, which was all the more disconcerting. Still, I could feel their presence.

My head was a blur of questions: How could I get away? How could I disable them? How could I possibly survive and then get back to my friends? How would I be able to do this before OP showed up with his army? Without any answers to any of these questions, I stopped before the shelves holding the five-gallon barrels of additives. I would have to stick to the one thing I could do, and then hope the rest would come to me.

"Okay," I said. "These," I waved both arms at the lower tier of barrels, "are the additives OP wants us to get."

Each glared at me, their eyes unflinching. Then I think it was my mute—because at this point, I couldn't tell which one was which—looked over to his brother, who just nodded to him, and then back to me.

That must have meant that they were waiting for me to do the heavy lifting. So I reached over and grabbed one of the small but heavy barrels and hoisted it up with a grunt. The damned thing must have weighed almost forty pounds, and I wasn't in the best condition at that point. Plus, it was bulky. I dropped it on its side, while fumbling with it. Then, figuring a lack of speed was preferable to injury, I rolled it down the aisle, back toward the exit.

"Shit!" I said after glancing back to see what the twins were doing. Each one had grabbed two barrels, one on each side, and were carrying both at once. And they weren't far behind me.

I pushed mine harder and faster, because I wanted to arrive at the vehicles before the brothers did. Outside, I picked the barrel up and lumbered purposely toward the second Humvee, the one that my mute's brother had driven.

Working to not drop the thing, I opened the back and hoisted the barrel inside, leaving the back open for the others. Just then I caught a glimpse of the key dangling in the ignition. And I believe I remembered the other one had left his key in the ignition of the Humvee we were in. They were obviously not too concerned about me making a run for it.

Both brothers showed up at the same time, and seemingly without effort, hoisted each barrel into the vehicle. I was out of breath and ready to pass out—more so from the stress of what was going on than the physical exertion. They stared and I got their ESP signal loud and clear: Keep moving!

So we did the next. And then the next after that. And then one more set of barrels.

Twenty barrels later, the three of us stood before the shelving units, confirming the bottom tier was emptied. And me still without any sort of plan about the other three shelves full of barrels above the emptied floor-level tier.

For just a flash, I considered trying to explain that the first tier was all there was, and that the others were different. But even without shining my flashlight on the barrels resting on the other shelves, it was easy to see these were exactly the same.

One of the two banged his pistol against my side and then pointed with it at the second shelf. He wanted me to go up there and pull them down next.

All I could do was sigh.

My flashlight told me the best path was on one side of the shelving unit, where a barrel was conveniently missing, and the next product was stored. I jumped up to the second level and the whole unit wobbled, threatening to send the entire load to the ground… On top of me.

Finally, I knew what I had to do.

With barely any hesitation, I skipped the second level and moved up to the third level, shining my light on each set of barrels. The whole shelving unit wobbled even more and so I held closer to it. On the fourth level, I pulled myself up and swung my feet around to face the twins below, bathing each of them in my light.

Both men glowered back at me, without squinting, and then at each other, obviously unsure what I was going to do next. Before they could act, I stuck the flashlight in my mouth, grabbed a barrel and hoisted it over the ledge, lowering it as far as I could, which was just below the third level. I dropped it.

One brother snatched it out of the air, as if I had tossed him a beach ball.

The next barrel was dropped with a little less agility, and I acted as if it had slipped from my grip.

This time, the same twin tried attempted to grab it with one arm, while holding the other, and dropped both. He cursed under his breath, though it sounded more like a grunt. Then he picked up both and walked easily down the aisle toward the doorway.

My next move had to be quick.

I stood straight up and flashed my light at the next one in line, and then the back of the shelving unit. It was as I had hoped.

Disappearing from sight, I pushed the next barrel over and it clunked against the hard cement. Immediately, I hopped to the back of the shelving unit, grabbed the edge of the back of the next unit and planted my feet against the edge of my unit and pushed with all my strength.

My shelving unit slowly leaned away from me. Then, with a back-breaking heave, I fully extended, sending the unit and all of its remaining barrels cascading forward with loud bangs like cannon fire. The entire unit hit the floor below with a thundering crash.

I had air for a moment and then I was dangling from the back edge of the other unit, suspended ten feet above the floor.

Quickly, I climbed down and directed my flashlight's beam at the collapsed unit. It was what I had hoped for.

In between the first and second tier were the legs of what I believed was my mute. The rest of his body was covered under the shelving. One of his legs shuddered, but just barely, as if the last impulses from his crushed brain were just making it to his extremities. I knew dead when I saw it.

But I wasn't going to wait around for the other brother. I bolted for the back of the warehouse and over one extra aisle, making my way to a different exit as silently as possible. After unlocking and checking for the other Twin, I exited and dashed around the opposite direction to get to the Humvees before he did. Even through the loud sounds of my trudging a path, I listened for the other brother, who surely wouldn't let me get away without a fight.

Both vehicles were still parked just as we had left them, but the last two barrels the other Twin had been carrying were abandoned in the snow, just before them.

I made a calculated risk and dashed for the back Humvee.

Reaching in the driver's door, I snagged the key from the ignition. Without closing the door or thinking what was the best strategy, I bolted for the front Humvee and at the same time, tossed the key off into the darkness.

This was stupid because I didn't know for sure the other key was even in mine.

But luck shined on me at that moment. It was there.

So I started it up, while glancing forward. It wasn't for any reason other than checking to make sure my way was clear and that I wouldn't run into the two abandoned barrels.

There in the glare of my headlights was the other brother, standing halfway between the building and my Humvee, holding the lifeless body of his brother in his arms.

Considering my blood must have been one-hundred percent adrenalin at that moment, it shouldn't have been surprising that my next movements happened before I could even think them.

The Humvee went into gear, the gas pedal punched in, and the steering wheel jacked to one side. The wheels reacted almost immediately, spinning wildly in the snow, looking for any sort of traction.

My eyes remained fixed on the live brother, watching what played out like a slow-motion action scene from a movie. Without any apparent effort, the brother laid his bloodied sibling down in the snow. When he rose up, he withdrew his pistol. Not even taking aim, he fired off shot after shot after shot.

The first one sliced a silent hole through the windshield and passed by my left ear. The second was slightly higher, but otherwise right on target, rocketing through the air just above my head. I don't know what happened to the third and subsequent shots as I was already driving away. But I could vaguely hear the ping sounds, like heavy rocks being hurled at the vehicle.

Every millisecond I waited for the pain to follow the gunshot that I knew was going to find its mark. But it never came.

I did have to wrestle control of the vehicle, which wanted to spin around and then back off the road in the other direction. Finally, I had it going straight and down the middle of the road from which we had come.

I bellowed out a breath that I must have been holding for several minutes, and then puffed in hitches, struggling to return some of the air my lungs demanded.

There was a trickle down my cheek, which I assumed was sweat, as I was as drenched as I would be after a run in the summer. But when I reached back to wipe my sweat away, something felt horribly wrong.

It was then that I knew I had been shot. Twice.

CHAPTER 35

Nan

Joey stuck a gag into Trout's mouth, and I applied the duct tape. Then he motioned that we go inside the house, out of earshot from both men. Joey wanted to talk, and so did I.

Chloe followed us to just outside the doorway, where Leticia was already sitting cross-legged with her back to the wall, holding onto Dog by his collar. She had left after Trout said he had listened to her admitting to shooting Buster.

"Honey, have you been listening to everything?" I asked and knelt down to face her.

She nodded.

"Well then," Joey began in a whispered tone, taking a knee beside us. "No sense leaving her out of the conversation, as she's already in it."

Chloe lowered herself to Leticia's level, as did I.

"What are we going to do now?" Chloe asked the sixty-four-thousand-dollar question.

Thankfully Joey answered, because I had nothing. "First, I'd like to know why Ron is being guarded by the two best hitmen in the Mexican cartel?"

Leticia's face was already welled up with tears, but after Joey asked this question, her wellspring burst open.

"Look," Chloe chimed in. "You scared her with that question. Maybe we should do this somewhere else."

"No!" Leticia said. "That's—not—it," she said in between sobs. She wiped her eyes and we waited for her to continue, because she obviously had something to say. "What if... What if Ronald joined forces with the bad men? And what if he always planned to abandon us?"

I gaped at her, stunned that she was thinking this.

"What?" was all Joey could say.

"Honey, why would you think that?" Chloe asked, oblivious to the signs Leticia and I had been seeing.

Leticia wiped at her face again and took a long breath. "Well, because of what I told you about Ronald taking the food and hiding it and the vehicle... But now because the fish man said that Polar Bear has two murderers protecting Ronald. And fish man said, Ronald is OP's 'golden boy.'"

Chloe put her hand on Leticia's shoulder. "Oh, Leticia. I really don't think Ron has changed sides. I would think he's just as anxious to get away from these bad men as we are."

"And consider," I said. "Every time Ron comes back, he's been beaten up by OP's men. And this last time, remember Trout, or as you like to call him, Fish Man, said that Ron was the one in trouble and that was why he was taken from us so abruptly."

I was not only arguing my point to Leticia, but to the others.

"And the best argument on his behalf is his stash. If he had sided with OP, he would not be hiding the supplies in a truck, in a hidden building. He's planning on leaving, all right. And I'd like to believe he's planning on leaving with us."

I glanced back and lowered my tone a little more, in fear that Trout or Matador could hear us. "And need I remind you, if it weren't for Ron, we wouldn't be here. And right now, he is probably fighting for his life against two psychopaths. The least we can do is stand up for him and give him a chance to explain. No, Ron is on our side and we need to do whatever we can to help him."

"Okay," Joey said anxiously. "Regardless of what Ron planned, we need to leave. Now. When OP and his men arrive, we won't have even that choice. We're all de..." He tossed a glance at Leticia. "Ah... we won't have any more choices then."

"Makes sense, but Joey's right," Chloe said. "We need to leave. We'll figure out what to do regarding Ron after..."

"I'm in agreement too," I said. "But what about those two: Trout and Matador?"

Joey glanced at Leticia, as if he were considering my earlier suggestion that we kill them, and then addressed me. "We leave them and walk out the front door."

I accepted his suggestion immediately. It was not as safe as killing them. But I'd already lost the taste for killing them.

"But where do we go?" Chloe asked the obvious question.

"Maybe..." I said. "If Leticia could help us find the building where Ron has his vehicle, we could wait there. And if Ron shows up, we can ask him what his plans are." I almost added 'if he doesn't show up, we can leave with his supplies.' But I couldn't bear that idea, so I didn't articulate it.

"Good thinking, Nan." Joey stood up. "Quickly, let's go to our rooms and put together a few things we can't live without and meet in the garage in five minutes. But not a minute longer."

We all rose and without saying a word, we made tracks away from the garden exit and headed to our rooms to collect the few things we could still call our own.

But with each step, the anxiety in me—and I'm sure each of them too—was building up to a panic level. Everything was on the line for us. And it would all happen in the next few minutes.

Unfortunately, we never made it to our rooms.

CHAPTER 36

Ron

The raw eruption of pain told me I was shot.

A simple motion of moving my right arm around my chest so that I could wipe away what I first thought was sweat, but turned out to be more sticky, caused an explosion of misery all around my bicep. That's how I knew I had been hit in two places.

After a moment of hyperventilating at this realization, I recognized that there wasn't any pain in my side. So perhaps when the bullet had passed through the Humvee's passenger-side, then into my arm, it hadn't hit anything else vital.

Then, as if to rebut my rationalization, the pain in my arm electrified and slapped me back to reality. If I didn't do something about my arm soon, I would certainly get weak and maybe even bleed out. But stopping the Humvee to do a proper triage and treatment probably wasn't an option: I had to keep moving if there was any chance of returning to my friends before OP and his men beat me to it. That was, if I wasn't too late. My gut told me I had minutes to get back. And I always trusted my gut.

Jamming my left knee into the steering wheel allowed me to yank the scarf from my neck with my uninjured arm. It could be used as a bandage. But even that slight movement escalated the shots of pain from my arm out to every part of my body.

"Dammit!"

My adrenaline was now waning, causing me to feel unbelievably fatigued. And with each percussion of my heart, I felt an urgency to stem my blood flow before it was too late.

You have to stop, or you might not make it back.

Giving in, my foot found the brake, slowing the vehicle to a stop.

With the Humee parked, I could focus on my wounds. I started by lassoing a knot just inside my bicep. This was pulled tight with my teeth on one end and my uninjured arm offering tension on the other. White lightning flooded my eyes from the agony. But I dared not pause, so I wrapped once around the wound and tied another knot around the other side of the damage. It would have to be enough for now.

My thoughts became soupy, while the white light burned even brighter.

Time for the other wound, I told myself.

Upon touching this with the hand of my uninjured arm, I grunted and screamed out a few profanities. The first bullet had not missed me entirely as I had first thought; it carved a section out of my cheek and my ear, both of which felt like raw meat. But I had nothing to dress and stem the flow from these wounds.

So even though the movement caused pain, my hand from my injured arm would have to be my temporary bandage.

Put more pressure on this, I willed myself. And I did.

Either I was running out of blood, or I wasn't bleeding as bad as I thought.

Still, the white light brightened.

Then I knew, it wasn't me.

It was headlights...

From the other brother's vehicle!

It took maybe three seconds to get my vehicle back into motion and headed in the right direction, when the other Humvee hit my rear bumper with the force of a freight train, sending me sideways.

With both sopping hands on the steering wheel, I corrected and punched down on the gas pedal, getting me back on track when he struck again. This time he sent me forward, rattling my body. This also shook some clarity into my thoughts.

I changed to manual to gain further control, and quickly shifted into a higher gear. Then I punched the gas once more, sending the vehicle up to a treacherous speed. This put a little distance between me and the oncoming Humvee.

I had barely a moment to think and wonder how this man could have found the key I had tossed into the snowy darkness, started up the Humvee and caught up, when he hit me again. This time, I held firm and was barely buffeted.

Up ahead was a turn.

If I slowed down, he would hit me with enough force to send me off the road. If I sped up, I would not be able to make the turn and would surely flip the truck.

So I did both.

I touched and held my foot on the brake pedal just enough so that my brake lights would go on and stay on, while at the same time I sped up. My pursuer tapped his brakes and slowed down, causing him to fall back behind.

The turn was in less than a hundred yards.

My foot came off the brake and I jammed in the clutch, while dropping the tranny into second gear. But I kept the clutch engaged and waited mere moments for my pursuer to bite.

He did.

Quickly, he closed the distance. When he was about to ram me, I let go of the clutch to engage the lower gear, while at the same moment doing a quick jig of the steering wheel, sending me to the left side of the road and then correcting the vehicle before it fishtailed and sent me spinning.

The other Humvee sling-shotted past me on my right, while I braced for the turn to my left. The red of his brake lights flashed like fireworks in the cracked windshield.

I hung on the wheel and tilted my whole body into the turn, my bad arm crying out. I think I was too. A little tap on the gas pushed me through the turn, while he shot off the road sideways and over into a tree on the other side.

But I wasn't out of it. My tail shuddered sideways and began to jog back around. I tried to correct in an attempt to bring it back. But I kept going around, as if the Satanic brother had somehow taken control of the vehicle anyway.

Afraid I would flip, I hit the brakes, and this sped me around the spin even more. The other Humvee flashed into view, and then disappeared as my spin continued.

It must have taken me around one more full revolution, because I came to rest pointed almost directly at my pursuer.

Either he was upside down or I was. I wasn't completely sure. My brain fog was back in full force, my pain the only thing keeping me conscious.

Letting go of the wheel, I waited to see if my arms would fall down or up. Both crashed into my lap, generating spasms of agony.

But for my hitching breaths, and the rumble of my engine, everything around me seemed quiet.

Maybe a hundred yards away, in between two bullet-caused spider webs in the windshield, my headlights caught movement.

It was the other brother. He was still alive.

His Humvee's windshield seemed to pulsate outward several times, as if it were convulsing out breaths like mine. Then the other brother's windshield shot out onto the snow. He had kicked it out.

From the truck's gaping hole, where the windshield was moments ago, the other brother crawled out onto the snow and stood up to reveal himself in the glare of my lights. I could see he was bloody, but it was impossible to know if that was his own blood or his brother's.

I shook my head in disbelief. He was like some sci-fi Terminator robot. Invincible. And I knew then that he would never stop coming after me. Ever.

Slowly at first, he began marching in my direction. Once again, he drew out his pistol as he approached.

There were only two choices for me: gas the engine and attempt to run him down, but he'd surely connect with a lethal shot this time, or I could turn the truck around and drive away from this maniac, as fast as I could. But I couldn't escape that easily from fate. I'd have to deal with him again, and if I didn't make it, Nanette and the others would have to.

There really was only one choice. And it was now or never.

Ignoring the pain, I placed both arms firmly upon the steering wheel and sighted the Humvee as if the truck and I were a giant bullet that I would fire at this otherwise unstoppable robot. I switched back to automatic, released the brake and gassed the engine. The robot-killing projectile was off, and it forced me back against my seat.

"Damn you!" I huffed and held tight to the steering wheel to keep us in a straight line.

The robot stopped in his tracks on the roadway, took careful aim and began firing his weapon.

Reacting almost as quickly, I eyed my target once more, before ducking below the windshield. My hands were the only thing exposed, still clasped to the steering wheel to maintain our trajectory. My foot pushed harder on the gas.

Everything went wrong.

A heavy object fell on top of me, then I lost control of the Humvee. I felt it slide and then spin. Finally, it crashed into something, and the world was silent.

I blacked out still clinging to the steering wheel, not sure if I got him or not.

CHAPTER 37

Nan

"It's OP and some of his men!" I announced.

A convoy of three big trucks had pulled up to the front of the house.

"Oh shit," I yelped into the front door eyepiece. "The shutters!"

We had left the front door unlocked and its corresponding shutter wide open so that Trout could easily breeze inside and get ensnared in our trap. But we had never secured either after we had so easily captured Trout. That meant OP and all his men could just waltz in.

Without thinking, I took a chance by yanking open the wood door, rushing over to the shutter, slamming it down and locking it up. Only then did I throw a glance out the shutter's view hole.

The sun's light had long since expired, as I felt we would if we didn't do something immediately. The wind howled indifference at our fate, as it did every day now.

I could vaguely see them. It appeared that no one had exited any of the trucks. So it was possible no one had seen me secure the front.

I made sure the wood door was properly secured, even though this would offer bare resistance if they breached the shutter.

Joey, Chloe, Leticia and Dog all swarmed around me in the living room.

"Listen," Joey said and held out either Trout's or Matador's radios we had taken from. He had the volume up and someone was demanding in Spanish that Trout or Matador open the doors and let them in. The voice also wanted to know why "the blond chick was free?"

"What now?" Chloe asked.

"Back—," I said, gasping.

"—Shutter," Joey finished, then dashed in that direction.

Dog barked enthusiastically, either in excitement because he thought we were playing a new game of chase or because he thought he might get to chew on some new bad men soon.

Joey was already dragging Matador backwards, still duct-taped in his chair, into the house when I joined him.

"Come on, Chloe. Help me get Trout," I said. We each grabbed a side of Trout's chair and carried him inside. I was going to suggest we leave them in the garden and just shut them out. But it was smarter bringing them in. They might be our only bargaining chips.

When Joey pulled down on the back shutter, with the intent of locking us in, I said, "Wait! Shouldn't we try and make a break for it? They aren't even out of their trucks because they think Trout and Matador are still in control."

Joey looked at me and then the shutter and then back at me, before he said, "How far could we go? We might be able to lull them in, or..."

He pushed the shutter back up and said, in a low voice this time, "I've got an idea. Can I borrow Dog?" he asked Leticia, who had been quiet the whole time. She nodded and guided Dog over to Joey.

"Go with me on this," Joey said holding a forefinger in the air before he clicked the button on the radio. "Hey boss," he said in his Matador gravelly voice. "Hold on a minute." He let go of the button and the speaker spewed a profanity-laced tirade in Spanish.

"He didn't like being told to hold on," I translated.

"Okay," Joey continued at barely a whisper. "I'm going to go out and pretend that we escaped out the back, by trampling the snow, leading out of the house into the bushes. Dog will tell me if anyone is approaching. We'll quickly circle back, returning the same way and closing the shutter behind us, unlocked. We'll be here before they pound the door in." He looked directly at me. "When I leave, tape up Trout and Matador's ears so they can't hear what we're doing. Then y'all quietly go to the secret room in the basement and wait for me."

He handed me Matador's rifle. "Here. You blast any sonofabitch that comes through your door unless it's me."

"Or Ron," I added.

"Right," Joey gave a small smile. "Now go."

He turned and said, "Come on, Dog, let's go hunting."

They darted through the garden and Joey once again sliced open both layers of the plastic covering the 2X4 structure that Ron never got around to finishing.

Because he was too busy planning his own exit slipped out of my mind.

When Joey and Dog left the garden, we shut the back shutter behind him, and the door, but didn't lock either. Just as Joey asked.

Trout and Matador mumbled angry things under their gags as we taped up their ears. Leticia watched from a distance. I also gave Chloe an extra strip and we each put one across their eyes as well. I figured blind and deaf was better than just deaf.

"Okay, let's go hide," I whispered to Chloe and then signaled this to Leticia. Without another word, we barreled down the stairs, through the basement, and into the secret room. We closed the secret bookshelf/door behind us, and we all huddled together at the little table. Well, two of us did. Chloe and I sat in the two chairs, while Leticia sat with her arms around her knees in Dog's bed. Her foot tapped a Morse Code of concern.

We had one of OP's radios, as well as one of our own —Joey had one of each too—on and we listened for what Joey's or OP's next move would be.

Barely a minute went by before OP's radio came alive with another flurry of Spanish. I was unfamiliar with many of the words. But the gist of it was, "Open up or we break down doors and shoot everyone."

CHAPTER 38

Ron

The robot brother's last bullet must have been fatal. Just not to me.

The Humvee was dead. Turning over the ignition elicited only a clicking sound, telling me the battery had a .45-inch hole in it.

A large portion of the windshield had collapsed inward, and was pressing down on me, pushing my body and head to the side. This was either from striking the other brother's body or from his rain of gunfire. Shouldering it forward, I was able to nearly put it back into place. With the extra room, I could sit up and attempt to figure out what had just happened.

The windshield was a thousand diamonds of violence with five perfectly round holes bored into it, all within a scary tight grouping about where my head should have been. By some unexplained miracle I had avoided getting hit again. I knew I was alive, because I still felt the same agonizing pain in my arm and face that I did before. And a new addition, the prickly bite of the cold nipped at everything exposed. That answered one question.

The next unknown that needed a quick solution: Did I run that maniac over or not?

Without a body, this was unanswerable. So my head was on an excruciating swivel, searching for any indication of where he might be.

That's when I saw movement out my side mirror.

It was him.

From the red glare of my brake lights, I could see him taking a stuttering step closer, followed by a long drag of a non-functional leg. One arm still clutched his pistol, swinging it forward with each lunging stride. The other arm appeared bent backwards at a disgusting angle. Either his featureless face was red from my brake lights, or it was completely covered in blood. But in the darkness, it was impossible to tell. I could only make out his two eyes, which glared holes into my mirror.

This was the most unbelievable person I had ever run across. Or in this case, run over. He really was a robot. And I had failed to stop him.

There was only one thing left to do.

Get out!

The handle rattled in my hand, but the door would not budge. Either it was blocked by the snow drift I had rammed into, or it was busted.

He continued to lumber closer.

My seat belt unclasped easily, and I slid onto the center console on my way to the passenger seat, just as the rest of the windshield released itself onto me, sending me back into my seat.

I had turned my head to avoid it, slamming the ruined side of my face down against the seat back. The side mirror revealed a glimpse of him passing behind the vehicle.

This time, I thrust hard against the windshield, pushing it all the way through the opening. It flopped forward onto the hood. I turned to my escape, pushing up from the seat.

Then I released myself back into the seat and let out a groan.

He was standing only a few feet from the passenger side window.

He had me dead to rights. There was no way I was going to escape this. But at that moment, I almost felt a sense of relief. I was tired of this fight. I wanted to be with Liz now.

He methodically ejected the spent magazine from his pistol and placed it firmly into his armpit. With his now freed hand, he jammed in a new magazine and re-clutched the pistol, while engaging the slide. A new live round slammed into the chamber. The round that would end me.

Then something surreal happened. The robot brother's face and body became more illuminated than before, as if he had his own internal light source and he turned it on just so I could better see him before he killed me.

His soulless eyes were locked onto mine, and his blood-covered face remained expressionless, the outlines of his lips almost imperceptible. Even though I couldn't read his face, it felt like the robot was satisfied that he was about to get revenge for his brother's death and for my making his job so difficult.

One final time, he lifted his pistol up, aiming it right at my head. I wanted to close my eyes and just accept my fate. But I couldn't pull my gaze away from his, like he was subliminally forcing me to bear witness to my own death at his hand. Then I saw it for the first time. A small curl of a smile cracked through his blood-soaked face. He would finally get his revenge.

But his smile instantly faded, and he shuddered, as if from an alternate realization.

It was the robot who broke the trance, turning his head slightly to the right, at the same time a large truck zoomed past my periphery.

They were both gone, as if neither had existed.

I turned in my seat to get a view out through the back of the Humvee.

The vehicle was an older model truck, which looked familiar, and had stopped some distance away. It did a three point turn and then slowly returned, with both its headlamps glaring at me. In between both of us, lay the motionless body of the robot brother. It looked broken and finally lifeless.

The truck's driver didn't seem to be taking any chances though, because he ran over the brother once more before gliding to a stop just beside me.

It occurred to me then why the truck looked familiar. It was one of mine.

I couldn't see much of the man who hopped out of the driver's seat, other than he wore fatigues. He appeared at the passenger side door and opened it.

In a voice I didn't recognize, he said, "Hi Ash. My name is Compton. Let's get you out of here and back home."

The rest of what happened was a fog.

Compton described himself as a friend. He said that he had been following me for a long time.

He shook me awake and I was sitting in the passenger seat of what I knew was one of my trucks. He had bandaged my wounds and told me that I had kept insisting that we get to the house as soon as possible.

Compton said nothing but pointed across me.

In front of Bob and Sarah's house, the place my friends and I had been living in these many months, a line of trucks idled. I knew then I was too late.

CHAPTER 39

Nan

Our fitful gasps for air were interrupted once again by OP's radio blaring.

Surprisingly, we heard what sounded like Matador announce, "Boss, they got away. Those pinche cabrones knocked us out and ran out the back garden. They left a minute ago."

This had to be Joey, but a seed of doubt made me wonder if it was actually Matador himself and if he did in fact break free. Joey—or Matador—was running at the same time as he was broadcasting. "I'm following... their trail down to the river. I think I see them. Hey, you..." There was a banging sound, a grunt and then nothing.

The radio erupted with someone who had a deep voice of authority, demanding to know, in broken English, where Matador went. Then there was a barrage of commands in Spanish for men to go in different directions, followed by vehicle doors slamming and other voices in the background.

I sincerely hoped that what we were listening to was evidence of Joey's great acting job. Because if it wasn't, then Joey was in trouble. And so were we.

There were footsteps upstairs. In response, Chloe and I turned down our radios to a dull murmur. OP's radio's light went on several times, indicating there were broadcasts. Most of it was in Spanish and indecipherable because the volume was too low. But we didn't want to risk it being heard.

Our own radio was the one we were more concerned with. Although OP's men had taken all of the radios we had been regularly using, Ron had found us two more. They were older but worked similarly to the others. We kept these in our secret room, but Leticia, while we were still interrogating Trout, had run downstairs and grabbed them—she must have known we were leaving then—to give Joey one and us the other. Now we watched for the light on our unit to flash, indicating that Joey was transmitting to us. But even then, I wouldn't dare take a chance and turn up the volume loud enough so that we could hear it. We would have to watch and wait.

Someone stomped away, with heavy boots near the basement doorway and then there was a clatter in the living room.

That was when our radio's light flashed.

Chloe reached over to turn its volume up. But I grabbed her hand, while holding a finger to my lips to tell her we needed to remain quiet regardless of what Joey was telling us. Just as I did this, we heard a tumble of footsteps coming down the basement stairs.

The footsteps grew louder, until they stopped right before the secret door.

We held our collective breaths and I lifted up Matador's rifle that Joey had given me to greet whoever was on the other side. "Assume the worst," Ron always said. I hoped it was Joey.

The secret door's lock clicked open.

As Joey had instructed, I flicked the rifle's safety off, and I prepared myself to shoot the next person who came through our door.

Joey popped his head in. "Just me." He didn't wait to see our reactions. But he probably heard all three of us sigh pretty loudly. Dog darted in right behind him, answering my next non-verbalized question. Joey swung the door closed and locked it behind him.

Chloe threw her arms around him. "Oh God, I was so frightened."

"Me too," said Leticia, wearing a face full joy as she roughed Dog's coat.

"Now what?" I asked, "Other than waiting them out."

"This is the hard part. We have to wait for them to search for us outside for a while, assuming Dog and I made our trail convincingly. Meanwhile, they'll come into the house and find Trout and Matador tied up and then they'll search the house. Of course, they won't find us. Eventually, they'll give up and they'll leave. When they do, we'll drive away,"—he held up Trout's keys to the truck Trout had arrived in—"and then we'll go try to find Ron."

What else could we do at this point? It was difficult to watch the seconds march by at a ridiculously slow pace. Still, we waited.

I turned up the volume ever so slightly on one of the two stolen radios and we listened to OP's men continue to talk back and forth, in animated voices, about their fruitless search for the gringos. The only joyful interruption to our endless wait was when we heard one of them had stepped on one of Ron's booby traps.

When Dog growled and we heard the creak of the floor above, I snapped off the radio.

❄ ❄ ❄

Trout

One of my hands came loose when I knocked over my chair. The whole thing cracked, and my hand was free.

Off came the tape that covered my eyes and my mouth, and one of the two covering my ears; the other piece which had covered my right ear had popped off because the younger chica did a poor job of it. This is why I knew that these gringos were up to some trick.

I hesitated over Matador, who seemed to know of my presence and angrily mumbled away, while rocking back and forth in his chair. But it wasn't time yet to let him go. He'd just get in my way. It was better having him tied up, and then releasing him later. I might even have some use for him. First, I had to figure out where these gringos were hiding.

This was most important. Because I was sure to see the end of OP's knife today, if I didn't figure out and solve this thing before any of his other men did.

I was always pretty good at reading people's lips and used this to my benefit many times. So when they first tied me to the chair and the chulo spoke quietly about what they should do next, I paid attention.

From the parts I picked up and the rest I could put together, their plan was to pretend to run away out the back and draw OP and his men away from the house. They would listen to one of our stolen radios or even broadcast using Matador's voice—which was very smart of that chulo—leading them farther away from the house.

This meant that they had to have a hiding place somewhere in the house, and my best guess was that it had to be in the basement.

I was about to check the basement when I heard someone come through the garden. I peeked out the doorway, because I wanted to make sure it wasn't the chulo or the dog, and instead it was Domingo, one of OP's men.

"What are you doing here?" I yelled at the man, who was not only twice my size, but was also known for being one of OP's top enforcers. Besides the Twins, he was the other one you didn't want to mess with. Add to this fact, Domingo was crazy.

"Why don't you answer your radio, pendejo?" he asked.

I ignored the put down and said, "I'm searching for something. Go outside and find them before the others so you can get your next medal."

For a job well done, OP often awarded one of his knives as if it were a gold medal. I won two of them over the years. This crazy guy had many more and carried each with pride. Today he wore a stupid looking mini-sword he got for cutting the throats of a rival gang's family while they slept.

"Only one of us will die tonight, and that won't be me," he said with too much hubris and marched back through the garden and outside to continue the search.

He was right, though. This was why I had to find Señor Ash's people's hiding place. I knew they were waiting us out somewhere.

After avoiding the broken pieces of wood created by that idiot Matador when he destroyed it, I stepped carefully down the stairs, stopping every so often to listen.

At the bottom, I looked around a place that I had been through more times than I could count. Then I had an idea. Above the lone table and chair, there was a pull chain with a single light bulb. It was what illuminated the entire basement space. I yanked the chain, sending the basement into almost total darkness.

Almost.

Then I saw it. At the back of the basement was just the slightest glint of light, jutting out underneath a bookshelf. There must have been a secret space behind it. That had to be where they were hiding.

But before I could do anything about it, I had to set this up.

There was a noise from someone else upstairs. I didn't want whomever it was to find Matador all tied up. Then I would have to also explain to OP why I didn't untie his idiot cousin.

This time, I hurried to the stairs and thought about my story.

Most important was that I get credit for finding where the gringos were hiding.

"Okay," I said midway up the stairs. I would tell this uninvited person that I had just uncovered their treacherous plot as we untied Matador. Then I'd have them go get OP and his men, and I would surprise the gringos and save my skin at the same time.

At the top of the stairs, I looked up and stopped dead in my tracks.

It was not who I had expected.

I opened my mouth to say something, and he hit me with the barrel of his small rifle, sending me to the floor.

CHAPTER 40

Ron

More electric shots of pain cascaded throughout my arm. But it felt so satisfying to drop Trout to the ground where that bottom-feeder belonged.

For just a moment, I considered delivering a kill shot, but then the robot brother's bloody image filled my head and removed that urge. Trout wasn't moving, and by the time he did, we'd be gone.

I wanted to avoid contact with any more of OP's men, having already slipped past two of them to get in unnoticed. Another had found one of my booby traps but wouldn't be telling any tall tales. I could hear at least two more outside and a crackly voice or two over radios. They were searching for someone, and this had made me doubly on edge. Could my friends have tried to escape already?

The tracks leading from the house seemed to indicate just that. But I had to confirm this, before going out and searching for them myself. And to make sure there were no further interruptions, I had yanked the shutter down and locked it behind me.

Encountering Trout and seeing the destroyed basement entrance had once again sent another bucket-load of adrenaline into my system. Somehow I needed to quiet myself and listen.

Other than Matador mumbling something under a gag and fighting his bindings—I hoped I would get a chance to hear how that happened—the inside of the house was deathly quiet.

I took the stairs one at a time, even though I wanted to run down them. The slushy prints pointed to at least one person having already come from the outside and down the stairs. The last thing I wanted to do was stumble upon another one of OP's men. At this point, I barely had the strength to hold up the AR pistol Compton had handed me.

Each step drew an agonizing creak. And with each step, I'd have to stop and listen before taking the next step. Creek, stop, listen and continue.

Finally, I was standing on the floor, eying the very back of the basement. The melting snow prints tracked directly there.

My AR pistol led the way. It may have been called a pistol, but it was more like a short-barreled rifle, with a pistol grip. Its weight made holding it difficult in my left hand, because my bandaged right arm was in a sling.

Just then, I recognized the weapon I was holding. It too was from my stash. It was a much shorter version than the rifles OP had taken from us when he invaded our lives. And besides being shorter, they were a stripped-down version, without any of the advanced optics; just flip up polymer sights. The one I carried, along with its other cousins, had been stored in my getaway truck that Compton had taken from me.

At this point, I had to trust the guy, even though after he had given me a gun I told him, "I should shoot you now for taking my truck and supplies." But he had saved my life, bandaged me up and, after all my apparent pleading, drove me here. Once he had possession of my stuff, he could have easily taken off.

With any luck, he would be still waiting for us when I returned with my friends.

Just before I addressed the bookcase doorway to the secret passage, I checked the basement once more to make sure no one was down there. Either my friends were there hiding in the secret room, or they had left.

I kicked the shelving unit with a boot, while holding the short rifle with my unsteady left hand. It was aimed toward it, just in case. "It's me, Ronald," I yelled. "I'm back. Are you there?"

Instantly replying was Nanette's muffled voice. "Ron? Is that really you—Wait, what are you doing? Let me through this door."

For a passing second, I wondered if Nanette was being held against her will, but the door clicked open and she leapt out of the secret room, arms extended.

"You're safe," she said, while attempting to wrap herself around me. But I stepped away before she could. "How in God's name did you break free from those two killers?" she added, and then reacted to my moving away from her.

I wondered how she knew about the two robot twins.

She then grimaced after catching a glimpse of my face and sling. "Oh my God. Are you—"

"—Never mind that for now," I interrupted.

"Dammit man, can't you stop getting yourself in trouble?" Joey twanged, as he emerged from the secret room with a smile.

"Are you all right, Ron?" Chloe asked, as she came out next.

Dog burst past them and barreled into me with all of his one-hundred-plus pounds, almost sending me down. He leapt up and woofed his delight.

"Down, boy. I missed you too, Dog," I said, uncomfortably trying to pet him with my rifle hand.

I caught a glimpse of Leticia, sitting in Dog's bed with her knees clutched to her chest, glaring at me. One of her feet tapped the floor percussively. I was going to ask what was going on with her, but there wasn't time. That was for later. If there was a later.

"I'm glad we're all safe, but we need to get out of here now."

A radio chirped and Joey raised his hand to reveal he was holding one.

A gruff voice spoke in one rapid-fire sequence. But because all but "OP" was in Spanish, I couldn't tell what they said. There was an almost instant reply, followed by another statement by someone else in even more indecipherable Spanish. I glared at Nanette, "What did they say?"

"The first one said something about finding a house by the river with a truck and supplies. Oh no, is that yours?"

"Not important. What else was said?" I asked but felt my heart sinking to new depths.

"Ah, I think someone said to come back. Then another was a request for... I think it was 'the two Juans' to respond."

Before we could even react to this, there was a pounding upstairs that sounded as if someone were banging on one of the shutters.

The feedback of a bullhorn sounded outside, and at the same time the radio in Joey's hand crackled.

"Attention gringos," a voice boomed. "You are to release our people and come out in the next two minutes, or we will burn this house down on top of you."

CHAPTER 41

Nan

"Well, so much for the 'get out of here now' option," I said.

Ron didn't say a word. He just darted up the stairs. Joey and Dog were in close pursuit. Chloe, Leticia and I followed as well, but slower. I felt like we were a line of mice, stuck in a laboratory maze, that was about to be blown up.

Ron halted at the top of the stairwell entrance and looked around. He was searching for something, or someone. He yelled something to Joey about Trout being gone. I wondered if he even knew we had him and Matador tied up in the living room.

Then I was upstairs and facing the living room, where I could see that Trout in fact was gone. Only Matador was tied up to his chair, whereas Trout's chair was broken and the strips of the duct tape we had used to secure and gag him were strewn about. He obviously escaped.

Joey announced from the front door's eyepiece, "They're pouring gas all over the house."

Ron was in the garage yelling for Trout to come out.

I carefully opened the wood door to see if we could still make a break for it through the garden. I tried to be quiet, but Chloe was right behind me holding back a handful of tears and then she shrieked, "Nan, are we trapped?"

Unlike the other two locked door shutters, in which Ron had cut out two round holes for easier viewing, this one had nothing. So I had to push up on one of the metal slats the quarter-inch or so that it would move and peek through the small opening this provided. What I saw took my breath away.

One of the garden's heaters that we always had on cast an eerie pale of light on the room. The room appeared empty, but just outside its translucent plastic walls, there was a silhouette of someone doing exactly what Joey had just announced.

They're getting ready to burn the house down with us still in it.

I slammed the door and just gave Chloe a vacant stare. Leticia slung her arms around my waist. Chloe had her back against the wall, with her arms wrapped around her heaving chest, eyes wet. She slid down the wall to the floor. She had given up. I felt like laughing, even though it wasn't appropriate.

Ron and Joey both returned at the same time. I wondered if Ron was going to do macho or compassionate. I didn't wait to find out.

"Oh Ron," I said, in an exaggerated Southern belle. "What shall we do?" Yeah, I don't know why Gone With The Wind came to mind at that moment. I guess humor was a cover for me.

Ron looked at me, and then he did something amazing. He smiled. It was genuine. He looked into my eyes and said first to me and then the others, "Don't worry, I promise you that we'll get out of this."

I had no idea what he was going to do. Or that there was anything that could be done. But he sounded so sure. So I became sure of this too.

He eyed Joey. "Better give me their radio."

Joey handed it over without protest, exchanging the radio for the rifle in Ron's hand.

Ron clicked the button and said slow and clear, "Hello El Oso Polar. This is Señor Ronald Ash. I am inside the house with your two men and the others." He let go of the button and looked at me. "Okay, now let's head downstairs."

No one moved.

The radio squawked, followed by, "Señor Ash? I am here, but I do not know why you are there. Where are the Twins?" It sounded like OP himself was responding.

"They're no longer of this Earth," Ron said very matter-of-factly.

"You are full of surprises Señor Ash. But you are also very valuable to me... You must come out now, with my two men and the little negra."

"What about my other friends?" Ron asked.

"I do not negotiate," he yelled. "You come out now or you all will die."

"You're not going to burn your own men, including your cousin."

There was no reply. OP had already said what he wanted to say, and it was obvious Ron knew it. He let the radio drop to his side. He seemed momentarily unsure about the next move, but then sprang to life. He then hollered at us, "Run to the secret room. Now!"

This time, we didn't hesitate. We dashed downstairs, me leading, dragging Leticia behind me. Chloe and Joey followed. Ron was slow walking down each of the steps, with his ear pressed against the radio.

My feet touched the concrete floor when I heard the radio blare down the stairwell, "Your answer?" It was OP.

We were already headed for the secret room, unsure why Ron was sending us to a place that wouldn't protect us if they burned the house down on top of us. Then I heard Ron respond.

"Nuts!"

CHAPTER 42

Compton

When the flames erupted, I was pretty sure they were done. Still I waited for them.

Several times I had considered leaving to go and help them. But I did not like the odds. There were far more cartel members swarming the house than there were members of Ash's group of survivors.

Further, I reasoned that if this group could somehow get out of this one, they would be even more hardened and better for me to hitch up my wagon. I had guessed incorrectly with the first group, none of whom were battle tested. And the results were obvious.

No, I had convinced myself if this group made it, they would be worthy of a man of my skills. Plus, no sense getting killed over this test. If they didn't make it, at least I had enough supplies to survive for a while, until I found the next group, as I headed South into Mexico, where I hoped it would be warmer.

I had high hopes for this group. They had found a way to scratch out an existence, even under the heavy hand of the cartel. They must have had skills that the cartel had found worthwhile, or they wouldn't have wasted any more of the world's dwindling supplies and would have simply exterminated them.

Like the Patriots, I found this group quite by accident. I was headed out of town after finding everyone in my group murdered. I was listening on the radio I had taken from the Mexican guard Ash and his partner had knocked out when I overheard the mention of some survivors in a house with lights on. I had been following them ever since, taking supplies when they weren't looking, keeping my distance.

I had just about given up on them as they allowed their cartel masters to suck away their will to fight, but when I saw Ash fight back against the two formidable men who were shadowing him, I knew I had to step in.

But even after field dressing his wounds, I wondered if I hadn't waited too long. Perhaps I should have approached them earlier—gotten them out of their predicament while they were stronger?

"No!" I declared to the empty truck cab. "One more test to prove they are worthy. If they pass this one..."

That's when I saw they were now ensnared in the one trap that was inescapable. It was what the cartel had done to my group too, during our standoff. They set fire to the house they were held up in, with them in it.

And like I did then, with my group, I now watched from a safe distance.

The flames quickly crawled up the walls of Ash's house and before I knew it, the whole house was consumed. There was no escaping this.

CHAPTER 43

Nan

What happened next seemed like a miracle. But it was just Ron.

I was still puzzling over his "Nuts!" reply. Even Joey asked him, "Nuts? What the hell is that supposed to mean?"

Ron ignored his question and marched past all of us, through the open door into the Hole. He stopped on the threshold, stooped over, and turned to look at all of us staring back at him like he in fact was nuts for saying this. We were hoping for something more, like a way out of here.

"Follow me and I'll explain," he said, and then stepped inside the room, clicking on the light.

We followed him inside.

Ron was standing before a large poster board, hanging on the very back wall of the Hole. It was a giant-sized poster art of the book cover for a novel called HIGHWAY, showing two young people walking down an eerie highway, with a mushroom cloud rising up in the background. We had never asked who put it there or why. Sarah had said it was one of her favorite books, and this piece of poster art, along with a couple of others, were up in her guest room. Some months ago, it had made it to this wall.

I glared at Ron, with what I could only assume was a look of complete bewilderment.

Ron began to speak. "General Anthony Clement McAuliffe had temporary command of the 101st Airborne division during World War II, when the Germans surrounded them near Bastogne. A German party delivered a letter to General McAuliffe, demanding his 'honorable surrender' or face total annihilation."

Ron turned away from us, clasped his only free hand to the poster board, awkwardly pulled it off the wall and set it aside.

Behind where the picture had been hanging was our miracle.

"The story goes," Ron continued, "McAuliffe read the surrender letter, crumpled it up and yelled what was to be their official reply, which was as follows:

"To the German Commander

NUTS!

The American Commander"

Ron smiled at each of us, with our mouths agape. "It seemed like an appropriate response. And the best part of it is Polar Bear will think we're all dead."

He turned his back to us and faced a rough-looking hole, obviously jackhammered out of the wall, which if I were to guess, led into Ron's basement.

It all made sense then: the secrets, the hiding the food, the vehicle he had hidden, always working on projects.

Ron put his foot on a little wooden bench pushed up against the wall—I had always wondered what that was doing there—and disappeared into the hole, his knees and hands making scraping sounds. A few seconds later, he hollered back, "Come on, Dog!"

Dog woofed his quick reply and bounded off the little bench into the hole.

A muffled, "Good boy," was immediately followed by, “Are you coming? It's going to get a little hot there soon."

We all laughed at this. Even Chloe.

Somehow, I ended up being the last person through. I guess my mind was slowly working through my amazement at Ron's achievement, along with the sheer relief that we might actually make it, when I noticed the secret room's door was left open. I ran over to shut it, but then stopped, thinking that it probably didn't make a difference because when the place burned down, it would bury the basement and all signs of our secret room and the tunnel to Ron's house.

I gave a quick glance out the doorway into the basement and caught movement. I froze and then saw the smoke. It was already pouring down the basement stairs. That must have been the movement I saw.

"I can see smoke already," I stated to the tunnel. Then I giggled at this, as if the fact that the cartel was burning our home down on top of us was funny. The whole thing was just surreal.

"Come on, Nan," Leticia yelled from the other side of the hole, her voice cracking just a little.

"Okay, I'm coming."

Into the hole I went, which wasn't concrete, except for the first few inches. It was patted down soil for about twenty feet, where a similar opening awaited me on the other end, along with Joey's hand. He helped me onto the concrete floor of what was obviously Ron's basement, on the other side of his basement workshop.

I turned to look back at this other secret opening, wondering why I never noticed it before. It too had a similar poster board, of some other book by the same author covering it. This one too was pilfered from Sarah's guest room.

"Come on," Ron said from the other side of the basement, where his own secret room was, supposedly leading outside, near the river. "We can't be sure they won't check here too."

That was true. We could unpack the questions about why Ron built this tunnel between the two houses and kept it a secret some other time.

When I approached the bookshelf opening to Ron's own Hole, I could already feel the cold. And when ducking through the entrance, I could see why. Just as Leticia said, there was another tunnel bored through the opposite wall, with a doorway leading to the outside. An Arctic blast of snow shot through, riding on a flurry of wind.

Ron handed me a winter coat—he thought of this too?—and ushered me through the opening.

Besides the onrush of air, the raging river sound was nearly deafening.

Chloe was on the other end offering her hand, while Joey was down below watching, holding Ron's short rifle. Leticia was behind him, and Dog was snuffing snow, seemingly oblivious to the screwed-up world around him.

"Isn't it crazy, Nan?" Chloe practically yelled.

"Yes," I mouthed, afraid someone would hear us if we spoke loudly.

"Put your feet right here when you come out." Chloe pointed to a log right below the opening.

I put one hand on the metal door to steady myself and one hand on Chloe's shoulder and hoisted myself out and onto the log.

Ron almost immediately popped out and I got out of the way.

Even though the door looked heavy, he closed it and pulled down on the latch with little effort.

I had to blink a couple of times, because it was so well camouflaged I had to really look to find any of the indications that something other than a mound of dirt and snow existed there.

Ron jogged down to Joey and pointed at some place in the woods, and Joey signaled for us to follow him. Ron went the other way. He wasn't wearing a winter coat, like the rest of us.

I did a sprint to Joey, because I had to know what Ron said and where we were supposed to go.

CHAPTER 44

Ron

It had to be below zero, and me without a winter jacket. I'm sure I could have found one later and made it back to Compton without freezing. But I wanted a little insurance for us, in case Compton wasn't who he said he was.

My hope was that OP's men had already given up the hunt and were now watching the great gringo weenie roast, because I had even less energy to get into a fight than I did when I walked this way only a few minutes ago. This time, I wasn't going all the way up to the house.

Even though the sky was moonless, and it was a perpetually cloud-filled night, I could easily make my way forward because of a new bright light that burned close by.

I passed by the trailhead which led to my yard and then bisected into Bob and Sarah's place that we had called home for several months. Just before the next trail up, I turned and trudged my way up the hill, through a thick snow drift.

I would have stuck my free hand into my pocket for warmth, but I needed it more for balance. If I fell, I'm not sure I would be able to get back up.

Halfway up the hill, I found what I was looking for.

After I had killed the oak-tree-sized guard, I had buried my bloody winter jacket, the guard's AK and my rifle. I found them right where I left them, wrapped up in one frozen bundle.

I laid the rifles down against a nearby tree and shook the jacket clean of snow and ice as best I could with one arm. This was swung around me, and I worked my free arm out, zipping it up over my slung arm. Although it was cold, my fading body heat quickly warmed it up.

I threw my rifle around my shoulder and onto my back, so it was out of the way. The AK pistol's sling went around my neck so that it rested in front of me. The charging handle was frozen solid. Using the tree and my weight, I was able to break it free, finally giving me the ability to cycle a round. It was ready to go, and I had planned to jog back to our group. But I held up.

I had to see.

So I trudged the rest of the way up, still listening for anyone coming my way. But there was nothing but the rush of wind and the crackle of fire.

At the break, I could see it. The entire home was engulfed in flames. Fire and sparks shot up into the sky. There were a couple of silhouetted figures with rifles walking around the periphery of the house. They must have been looking for one of us to escape. But their movements were slow and controlled. This was probably because they had found one of their own killed by one of my booby traps. Plus, they knew no one could have made it out of the house alive. I wasn't about to prove them wrong.

I sneaked down the hill and returned the way I had come.

When I walked past the point of my secret basement exit, I noticed something looked off. The outline of the door was visible, even though I built it to be invisible.

Ron, you idiot. Did you forget to latch it? I castigated myself.

But I knew I had.

My hand constricted around the AK's handle, and I swung the barrel forward and eyed the area around me. It occurred to me that I hadn't checked the safety, and after fiddling it for several long seconds, I was able to click it to the "fire" position.

I pivoted on a heel and searched a good three-sixty around me.

There was no one and no sounds, other than the roar of the Guadalupe.

When I pushed down on the latch, it sealed the door and the whole thing became nearly invisible again.

"Weird," I said to myself. "Come on, Ron. Get moving."

And so I did. But I had that horrible feeling that once again, I wasn't alone.

CHAPTER 45

Nan

"What did Ron say?" I asked Joey.

We were all waiting in a gully of deep snow, maybe a hundred yards from the place we turned away from the river. Poor Leticia and Chloe were freezing. Joey and Dog seemed unfazed by the cold, much less the events of the day.

I was about to repeat my question, when Joey leaned toward me and whispered, "Ron asked me to lead us to this point and wait for his return. He said we are to keep quiet, and he would explain our next move after he got something he said we would need."

He held a hand up when I was about to ask him a follow-up question. "Nan, that's all he said. So don't ask me anything else; you know as much as I do." Then he proceeded farther up the gully, to talk to Chloe.

What more could I say? Ron once again had been two steps ahead of everyone. And we would have to wait if we wanted more information.

All our heads snapped toward the direction we had come when we heard some noise coming up from the river. Joey slogged back down the incline toward me. He had Ron's gun, which was the only weapon between all of us, as we had forgotten Matador's rifle and Trout's pistol during our escape from the house.

He stopped just past me, pointing at the murk, with the short military-style rifle.

We held our breaths for a long period of time.

I tried to whisper, "Do you—"

But Joey cut me off with a hand thrust in the air—his way of saying, "Shut up, Nan."

He was right, of course, no matter how annoying the gesture was. I heard the noise too... But now nothing.

We sat there in the snow, freezing our keisters off, when there was another noise. Almost immediately, we could plainly see it was Ron coming up the gully to meet us.

He was wearing his large winter parka that had mysteriously disappeared earlier. And now I understood why: It was covered in brown-red smears of blood.

I never had the chance to ask Ron what had happened. But based on Leticia's description, this must have been the blood from the missing guard that Ron had killed. Ron must have hidden this in the snow before coming back, when Trout and Matador were waiting for him. He also had two rifles slung around him.

He whispered something to Joey, who nodded and then helped to relieve him of the longer rifle he had been carrying. Ron then walked up to me and whispered, "I'm going to lead us forward to the road that connects with our subdivision. Please keep quiet and pull up the rear with Joey, who will give you a rifle. I need you to keep your eyes open and be prepared to shoot if you have to. We're almost home free."

He clasped his ice-cold hand around one of mine and attempted a smile. But his effort at being calming seemed a struggle. It had the opposite effect on me.

He then trudged past me to Chloe and Leticia, where he whispered to them.

I had so many other questions, like where we were going, now that OP's men had found his stash and getaway vehicle? Or why he never bothered to tell us about the secret tunnels? Or was someone following us? But there was no time to ask them. I wondered if there ever would be.

There was a light tap on my shoulder and Joey said in a quiet voice, "Nan, let me show you this."

He held up the short rifle Ron had given to him earlier.

"This is an AR-15 pistol. It holds thirty rounds and is more accurate than the cannon you were carrying earlier." He flicked up two metal-looking pieces on the top of the weapon and I could see they were for sighting it in. "These are your sights." He demonstrated how to look through them. "You flick the selector to "Fire" here when you're ready to shoot." He showed me the lever. "But keep your finger here and don't put it on the trigger unless you intend to kill the person in front of your barrel. Do you understand all that I have just told you?"

While I nodded, he slipped a sling around my neck and my right arm and released the weapon to me.

I had to admit, I really liked the feel of this one. It was like a pistol, but was also like a rifle, and the sling took up most of its weight.

"Nan," Joey said so lightly, I almost thought it was the wind in my ear, "I'm going to follow far behind to make sure no one is following us. So please don't shoot me and don't panic if you don't see me. I've got your back. Now get going. Ron is taking us forward."

I nodded and turned to see that Chloe and the others were walking and already a dozen yards away.

I looked back and Joey was gone. Something dug at me inside, and I couldn't shake the feeling that I would never see Joey again.

CHAPTER 46

Ron

Joey was told to expect the worst, because I did not know what was going to happen next. Only that something was coming.

He needed to hold back out of sight and make sure no one was following behind. But I also asked him to watch for any sign that Compton, our new friend who was supposed to be waiting for us, was potentially not on our side. I didn't have time to explain why I felt the way I did, only that I couldn't help thinking that we were being set up, that Compton was going to screw us in the end.

Joey, to his credit, didn't flinch. He was unflappable, rarely allowing anything to affect him. So when I told him all of this, he just nodded and then proceeded to do what I had tasked him to do.

I, on the other hand, felt so sure that something bad was about to happen; everything felt wrong. Our escape felt too easy. While returning to pick up my coat and weapons, I expected to see at least one of OP's men outside of the burning house's perimeter or around my house. But there was no one. Then there was the sense once again that I was being followed... My already edgy mind took every noise or moving branch and turned it into one of OP's henchmen about to burst out of the dark and start shooting all of us. If I were bringing up the rear, like Joey, I'd probably have gone crazy.

I moved our group up a small gully that bounded my property and another. One tentative step after another, we moved as quietly as we could through the snow, while being hyper-aware of anything and everything that might be a threat. In maybe a hundred more yards, we would exit onto the residential street where Compton had parked covertly before letting me off. He said he would be waiting for us there. Would he be gone, or would a band of OP's men be waiting there for us instead?

We had no other choice. Once it was announced on the radio that OP's man had found my hidden garage, along with the other bug out vehicle and the rest of our supplies, Compton became our only salvation.

It occurred to me then that I couldn't tell if my only free hand was still holding onto the heavy AK that I had taken off the big guard earlier. My arm shuddered from its monumental weight, but I couldn't feel my hand. So I looked down and squeezed harder onto the pistol grip, just for confirmation. The lighter AR pistol would have been preferable to this one, but I was afraid that Nanette would not have easily been able to fire this gun after it had been frozen in the snow and ice for most of the day. At this point, I wasn't sure I'd be able to make the damned thing work because I was just as frozen. But for my wrapped-up wounded arm, I'd lost most of the feeling in my extremities long ago. That was except for the telltale signs of frost bite.

Get over it, Ron, at least your gunshot wounds don't hurt as bad now.

But oh, my feet did.

Each footstep in the snow generated excruciating pinpricks, as the cold had long since wicked its way into my skin and bones, killing more skin and muscle tissue than I cared to guess.

But none of that mattered. Even if all of this ultimately killed me, I had to get my people to safety. Now, it came down to this: If Compton was there waiting for us, we would all have some time to breathe and get warm, and I could pass out. If he wasn't there waiting for us, nothing that preceded this mattered: my wounds and their corresponding pain, my wife and my friends dying, my being forced from my home... All of this loss would have been for nothing if Compton wasn't there.

Just ahead was our destination: the break in the trees, leading onto the road.

I halted.

Bright headlamps from a vehicle up on the road momentarily bathed our area in light.

I knelt in the snow and held up the AK to signal the others. The headlamps' glare, muted only by the snow-covered foliage of the trees lining the street, moved forward, and then past us. Because of the wind, I couldn't tell what kind of vehicle it was. Only that it was headed away from our neighborhood.

My mind raced as it tried to guess if this was Compton, taking off with my truck, and our only chance of survival. Or was it someone else?

I jumped up and quick-stepped the last few feet. But I had to temper myself, in case it was one of OP's vehicles, and there were others—or worse, his men were just waiting for us to pour out of the woods.

At the break, I stuck my head through the foliage and turned to examine the road where I should have seen Compton.

The truck is gone!

A full-on panic hit when I turned to look in the other direction. The taillights of the vehicle I had seen moments ago were nearly a mile away, and about to turn from our road for good.

Game over, Ron!

I lumbered into the road and just stared at the red lights as they disappeared.

At that moment, I felt a dual sense of absolute loss and extreme anger. I was torn between wanting to just let myself fall onto the road and give into the cruel cold, or running down our street and killing every sonofabitch cartel member I could, before they got me.

I was about to choose the latter when the face of each of my people gleamed in my mind. They were relying on me. I couldn't fail them, even if everyone else did. Even if Compton left, as long as I could take in a breath, I would find a way out of this.

I caught a flash of something in my periphery.

As I swung my body a quarter turn, my finger found the AK's trigger. But I wasn't sure how hard I would have to pull on it to make it work.

This time I saw the flash more clearly. Another tap of brake lights, under the canopy of a tree.

But from this glimmer, I could make out the outline of a Land Cruiser. And I heard the familiar sound of its engine firing up. It was Compton.

I let go of the pistol, allowing the sling take all of its weight and waved the rest of our group to come on up to the road.

Compton pulled the truck up to me and rolled down the window. "Would you like a lift?"

I couldn't help but let a smile explode on my face.

"What did you think, I'd leave you after all that?"

All I could do is nod and say, "Yeah, I did."

"Well, there were quite a few doings around here. When you left—"

I held up my hand. "Sorry, but can you save it for when we're all out of here?"

"Yeah, sure. You wanna drive?"

"Yes, and can you introduce yourself and help everyone into the truck?" I asked.

While he did that, I yanked the fuses for the back brake lights, taillights, and interior dome lights. Did not want those to go off and signal our existence in the dark. I climbed up into the driver's seat and laid the AK in my lap, while I waited for everyone to get in.

And yet I felt no joy.

Each second crawled by, while everyone moved in slow motion getting Compton's introduction and instruction. Meanwhile, I eyeballed the rear view and side mirrors, as well as the front windshield, still absolutely sure that OP himself or his men would appear at any moment.

CHAPTER 47

Nan

"Hello, my name is Compton. I'm a friend," said the stranger, who introduced himself and then guided us to a vehicle I had also never seen before.

Ron was in the driver's seat, which brought me some comfort. But I could see he was still on edge, and I couldn't shake my own uneasiness. We weren't out of this yet. That I was sure of.

I looked behind me for a moment to see if Joey was there, but he wasn't. Then my eyes were drawn to the orange and white glow directly behind the trees. I knew this was Bob and Sarah's place—our home—burning to the ground.

I felt instantly anxious about our sitting here in the road, while OP's men were in front of our house. If any of them were to turn out of the cul-de-sac onto this road, they would see us. And that would be our end.

I eyeballed the man who called himself Compton as he was getting some instruction from Ron from the open passenger door. Compton then pointed Leticia and Dog into the front seat, and then closed the door.

Compton slipped into the back seat with me, and Chloe tentatively followed, leaving the door open.

"What about Joey?" I asked.

Ron stuck two fingers in his lips and whistled.

A few seconds later, Joey hopped out of the brush and into the packed truck. And we sped off.

Ron pointed us down the middle of the road without headlights. We were jammed in the back: Joey with Chloe on his lap at one end, this complete stranger named Compton in the middle, and me at the other end with my weapon pointed out.

What if Compton turned out to be a bad guy? My mind begged the obvious question. There was no way I could turn my weapon around and use it on him.

You idiot, my brain yelled.

But he had to be good. He waited for us this whole time. And somehow Ron knew him. Even Dog seemed to approve of the stranger, and Dog appeared to be a good judge of character. It was not like we had any other choice.

I turned in my seat to look out the back. It was dark directly behind us, as our taillights were off. Then the trees cleared, and our cul-de-sac came into view. Or rather our house did. It was completely engulfed in fire, one side leaning inward about ready to give way

"Look," I said mesmerized by the sight.

Quickly it disappeared as we put distance between us and them.

Ron swung us south, down the road leading out of town. Then almost immediately, we swung right, into a side street. We parked beside a building, shielded from the road.

Ron turned in his seat to face us but didn't say anything.

"So boss," Compton spoke, "are we going back to the garage for the other vehicle?"

"What other vehicle?" I asked, thinking what we were in was it. But then I groaned as I remembered the radio announcement about OP's man finding the pickup truck, full of supplies. We are not going to do that, are we?

"And from what we heard on the radio," Joey said, adjusting Chloe on his lap. "It's only a mile away from here, right? Plus, if there is anyone there, it's probably only one person."

"I'm all for it." Chloe added, "It would sure make it easier if we were spread out in two vehicles rather than crammed in just this one."

Ron looked down and grunted, his face contorted. He was either in a lot of pain, or this discussion was bringing him agony too.

Finally, he looked up. "I just didn't want to run into any more of OP's men. I'm not sure I can physically handle another skirmish. I can barely stay conscious at this point."

"Why don't you let me worry about that?" Joey said.

"I can help too," Compton said.

"Don't forget Dog," Leticia stated from the front.

Ron swung back in his seat and announced, "All right. I guess we have one more stop to make before we finally leave this place."

CHAPTER 48

Ron

The building looked empty. But the door was left open, and not by me.

We parked across the street, so we could see the garage, but far enough away that we wouldn't be easily seen if OP's men were there or showed back up.

"Are you sure—" I started to say to Joey.

"No, I got this," Joey interrupted and then opened his door. He whispered to Chloe to be quiet and to go back into the truck when Compton was out.

She timidly agreed and waited for Compton before hopping back in.

Joey shut the door behind her so quietly I almost didn't hear it.

I watched from the mirrors as Joey and Compton checked their weapons and then headed to the garage.

Compton had offered a brief, but impressive explanation of his military experience as a SEAL. He insisted that he should do a once-around the perimeter of the building before Joey entered. When Joey asked why he thought he would be more covert, Compton said, "Well, I watched you two trying to collect intel on the cartel's compound, while neither of you knew I was there."

When we had grumbled disbelief, he offered a description of my Cubs hat, how the big-as-an-oak-tree guard caught me and how Joey knocked him out as further proof.

I watched Compton dash to the side of the building with the agility of a twenty-year-old, while Joey slowly approached from the other side, nearly invisible.

By the time Joey was nearing the doorway entrance, Compton was there. Neither man seemed jumpy, whereas I was a bundle of nerves.

Joey flicked on the flashlight attached to his rifle barrel and stepped inside the garage. Compton gave us a thumbs-up and disappeared inside.

"Do you think there's anyone there?" Leticia whispered. She had slid closer in her seat and peeked around me.

"I don't know," I said. "Let's be quiet until we see them come back out. Okay?"

Dog, who had been laying his mug on Leticia's lap during all of this, offered a muffled groan. He hated not being in the action. But he wasn't the only one.

Nanette rustled in her seat, playing with the AR pistol that she refused to relinquish. She had offered to go out there too, but I suggested we best leave this operation to the two military guys. One thing I'll say, this woman had guts.

The wind whipped furiously at the truck, jostling us inside. Yet we remained utterly silent.

I considered getting out when the large garage door lifted up. Compton appeared on the other end of this, pushing it all the way up to reveal two trucks: one covered, in the back, and one pointed forward, ready to drive out.

There had been three: the Land Cruiser that Compton had taken earlier and two older model pickup trucks. One of them I never had a chance to work on, whereas the other I had purring like a cougar, and packed to the point where it was overflowing with supplies.

The stuffed pickup moved forward, with Joey behind the wheel, and exited onto the street, in between us and the garage. Compton pulled the garage door down and exited the door he had come in, pulling it closed as well. He then dashed up to our vehicle and entered in the back, slamming the door behind him.

"Okay," Compton said, "we need to get out of here quick and then park maybe a mile away. Joey said he'll follow behind us."

"Got it," I said, and put us into gear.

We turned back on the main road, going south, and took it for about a mile. And as Compton directed, we pulled off the road and parked.

Joey was right behind us. He parked the pickup and dashed forward to us. Compton opened up the door for him to slide in.

After Compton closed the door, but for Joey's heavy breathing, no one uttered a peep.

"Why are we parked here?" Nanette asked.

I wondered the same. But I knew I had to trust that Joey and Compton knew what they were doing. And for once I relished the fact that someone else had done the planning.

"Wait for it," Compton said, as he glared out the driver's side back windows.

"It was Compton's idea, and I think it's a good one," Joey offered, his head also turned and staring out the back windows. "He said, 'you know if we take this truck, they're going to know it.'"

I had to ask. "So what did you—"

A flare of light burst out of the darkness a mile away, followed by an orange and red glare. A second later, there was a muffled boom.

We gawked at this for a few seconds before Compton explained. "You had a barrel of fuel, and some flares. I just set up a timed explosive. By the time the cartel gets there, it will be rubble."

"And one burned-out pickup truck," Joey finished. "And with any luck, the man who reported it will not remember there were two there."

"Won't someone wonder why it exploded if we all died in the house fire?" Nanette asked.

"No," I answered. "They'll think I had set up a timed booby trap that was set off after one of them entered."

"Why would they think that?" Nanette asked.

"Because I suggested that very thing to OP as a theft deterrent."

"So we're home free?" Chloe asked.

"I think so," I said. And I believed it. "We are free to go anywhere we want now."

Someone was crying and I turned to address her. "Hey-hey, what's wrong, Leticia?"

"I-I thought you were leaving us. I didn't know..." She hung her chin on her chest and sobbed.

"I'm so sorry, honey," I said. "I had always planned on leaving with all of you. You're all my family now. So I'm only going where you're going. But I'm sorry that I held onto so many secrets and didn't tell you." I looked up at the others. "I thought I was protecting you all by not telling you everything. But I know it was wrong not to trust you. And I'm sorry."

Leticia looked up, her eyes still leaking, but her sobbing had stopped.

"Will you forgive me?" I asked.

She nodded yes and wiped at her face with the backs of her hands. I looked at the others and they nodded. Nanette's eyes were watery too.

Compton sat quietly, giving us the time we needed.

But I felt too conspicuous out there and wanted to leave. "Okay, we have enough gas to get both vehicles about 600 miles from here. So where are we going?"

Everyone had an opinion. Leticia argued for a place called Blackstone in Wyoming. She found them on the radio because they were asking for people with skills to join them. Joey reminded us that his family had a ranch in Arizona, and that "everyone was welcome." Compton told us before he decided to help us, he had planned to go to Southern Mexico, where it was hopefully warmer, and he knew someone with a big tract of land on the coast, where we could fish.

I have to admit Compton had me at the mention of fish. "Okay," I suggested, "how about this? Let's head to Arizona, and Joey's family's ranch. I think we can make it with the gas we have. Meanwhile, we'll talk about it and together decide on whether we want to go to Wyoming or Mexico by the time we reach there."

"Mr. Compton, if you're coming with us, can I interview you for my book?" Leticia asked.

"Sure, kid," he said with a chuckle.

We agreed to split up, with Joey and Chloe leading by driving the pickup truck and the rest of us in the Land Cruiser. I asked Nanette to drive, because I informed her that I needed to pass out pretty soon. Nanette asked if I could hold her AR pistol while she was driving, but that she wanted it back. I didn't tell her that there were others in a case in back.

"What are you smiling at?" she asked.

"Oh, nothing," I replied.

Once we were driving, Leticia had already started interviewing Compton, who seemed to be pretty free with his story. Most surprising of all of this was Dog. He had joined Leticia and Compton in the back seat. Dog, who could be terrifying if he didn't like you, had rolled over on his back and was almost asleep as Compton stroked his belly.

In spite of all that Compton had done to save us, it was because Dog accepted him that I knew Compton was all right. If Dog trusted him, then I would too. I think Liz would have liked him too.

I smiled at this and closed my eyes, letting her foggy image appear in my head.

I wanted to listen to all that Compton said, but I was just too exhausted.

I turned my head and stretched my legs out to get more comfortable, knocking something off the seat. I caught a blink of light and my heart skipped. And I realized it was one of OP's radios. The light had gone on, indicating that someone was transmitting on that frequency. I knew I should have probably listened to this. But at this point, I just didn't care. That part of our life was now in the past. So I clicked the radio off to save its battery and stuck it in the center console.

Compton was telling Leticia how he found the survivor's group he was with, when I returned to my thoughts of Liz. I hoped she'd be the star of my next dream and we could talk as we had in previous dreams. I wanted to tell her how much I missed her. I wanted to find out what she thought of Nanette, and Joey, and Leticia, and Chloe, and now Compton. I wanted to...

EPILOGUE

Interrogation of Silas "Trout" Guzman - Recording #62

Yeah, so when I heard about the truck and supplies, I knew they belonged to Señor Ash. And even though one of our guys had found them, I knew Señor Ash would return to them. I just had to get there first.

After he had surprised me at the house, my choices became pretty simple: It was either meeting the sharp end of my boss's knife or burning to death. Neither were choices at all. That left finding a way to catch Señor Ash and his group before they got away.

His return to the house that OP was about to burn down was Señor Ash's admission that he had set up some sort of tunnel out of there. Otherwise, his return was suicide. There was no other way for them to escape. My guess was that it was accessible from the basement, from their hidden room. All I had to do was hide in the basement and wait for them to show me the way. They did exactly this, leading me out before it all burned to the ground on top of me.

Then I had to find the garage.

Hector was the one who announced finding Señor Ash's garage and truck full of supplies. Hector was afraid of his own shadow and so he would not have waited for anyone else to arrive while he was there. He would have left and returned with help. Meanwhile, OP and his men would be too preoccupied with burning Señor Ash's group alive in their house, and not letting any of them escape from its regular exits. No, they would go to the garage much later. Probably the next day. So as Señor Ash and his group scurried away into their secret hole in the ground, I would follow behind until they got to the garage. But then they did something unexpected.

They turned off the trail and walked behind the property. I figured they must have had some other vehicle ready close by and they would come back to the garage for the rest of their supplies after they got away. It was a bold move on my part, but all I had was the radio and my intellect to tell me what to do.

So I only had to find the garage, slip in and wait for their return. Simple.

Hector was not particularly smart and must have stumbled upon it. So I guessed it would be just off the trail and not too hard to find. In fact, it was pretty easy. I was just amazed that no one had found the place before him. Of course, this made sense, because most of OP's men were stupid.

Hector announced there were a lot of supplies, and he wasn't kidding. There was enough food and supplies to last one or two people a year or more. And for just a moment, I thought about taking it all myself and leaving OP. But where would I go? What would I do? I preferred to follow a strong leader and make myself invaluable to him. OP was my best choice.

So to be invaluable to OP, and save my skin at the same time, meant I had to catch Mr. Ash and his group when they came for their supplies. If I did that, after OP had thought they had been killed, maybe I would be given the respect I deserved. And not just from OP, but from all of his men too.

I was in the garage, considering my options, when I heard a vehicle drive up.

There was an opening in the tarp stretched over the pickup bed. Just underneath, there was room for one person. If I could crawl in there and close the tarp over me, I'd listen for Mr. Ash. When I heard him, I would call OP and let him know where to find them.

The area in the pickup bed was adequate. And lashing up the tarp tight from inside was easy enough and would make it difficult for someone outside of the truck to loosen it.

So I waited.

First in was Chavo, and then someone whose voice I did not recognize. They discussed how they would take the truck, join up with Mr. Ash and the rest of the group, and then burn the garage down, as if it were a timed device that was set off by accident from Hector finding them.

I would have called OP on the radio then, but they were too close and would hear me. I would have to wait a little longer. But I wasn't worried then since I was in the truck with all of the supplies. Señor Ash was going to come to me... If I did not freeze to death first.

After too long, while Chavo drove the truck, he parked and left me and the pickup unattended. I undid the tarp and checked. Everyone was crammed into a larger vehicle, in front of the pickup.

It was time.

I pulled out the radio clipped to my belt, just as the Chavo returned with the pretty blond.

Pendejo, I cursed and slipped in and pulled the tarp back over me again. I'd have to broadcast while we were driving.

I put the radio to my mouth and transmitted what I thought was my location and that Señor Ash and his group were alive and escaping. I didn't know if I reached anyone. But it was on the common frequency OP and his men were using, so I'm sure someone heard. They should be able to find us easily enough. After all, how many vehicles were driving around now, during an Ice Age?

Thank you for reading!

Find out the exciting conclusion in ASHFALL APOCALYPSE 3

Did you like Ashfall Apocalypse 2?

Help spread the word about this book by posting a quick review on Amazon and Goodreads.

Reviews are vital to indie authors like me. If you liked this book, I would really appreciate your review.

Thank you!

Want another free Ashfall Apocalypse short story?

Compton, a Navy SEAL, and savior of Ronald and his group in the Ashfall Apocalypse saga, has a fascinating backstory. Find out what happened to Compton before he saved the day and something disturbing, which may affect everyone's future in this short story titled, Compton's Epoch. Download a free copy of this exclusive short, not available anywhere else, to learn more about one of Ashfall Apocalypse's more colorful characters.

https://www.subscribepage.com/ashfall2

Who is ML Banner?

Michael "ML" Banner is an award winning, USA Today Bestselling author of Apocalyptic Thrillers

Michael writes what he loves to read: apocalyptic thrillers, which thrust regular people into extraordinary circumstances, where their actions may determine not only their own fate, but that of the world. His work is traditionally published and self-published.

Often his thrillers are set in far-flung places, as Michael uses his experiences from visiting other countries—some multiple times—over the years. The picture was from a transatlantic cruise that became the foreground of his award-winning MADNESS Series.

When not writing his next book, you might find Michael (and his wife) traveling abroad or reading a Kindle, with his toes in the water (name of his publishing company), of a beach on the Sea of Cortez (Mexico).

Want more from M.L. Banner?

MLBanner.com

Receive FREE books &

Apocalyptic Updates - A monthly publication highlighting discounted books, cool science/discoveries, new releases, reviews, and more

Connect with M.L. Banner

Keep in contact – I would love to hear from you!

Email: michael@mlbanner.com

Facebook: facebook.com/authormlbanner

Twitter: @ml_banner

Books by M.L. Banner

For a complete list of Michael's current and upcoming books: MLBanner.com/books/

ASHFALL APOCALYPSE

Ashfall Apocalypse (01)

A world-wide apocalypse has just begun.

Collapse (02)

As temps plummet, a new foe seeks revenge.

Perdition (03)

Sometimes the best plan is to run. But where?

MADNESS CHRONICLES

MADNESS (01)

A parasitic infection causes mammals to attack.

PARASITIC (02)

The parasitic infection doesn't just affect animals.

SYMPTOMATIC (03)

When your loved one becomes symptomatic, what do you do?

The Final Outbreak (Books 1 - 3)

The end is coming. It's closer than you think. And it's real.

HIGHWAY SERIES

True Enemy (Short)

An unlikely hero finds his true enemy.

(Get this USA Today Bestselling short only on mlbanner.com)

Highway (01)

A terrorist attack forces siblings onto a highway,

and an impossible journey home.

Endurance (02)

Enduring what comes next will take everything they've got, and more.

Resistance (03)

Coming Soon

STONE AGE SERIES

Stone Age (01)

The next big solar event separates family and friends,

and begins a new Stone Age.

Desolation (02)

To survive the coming desolation will require new friendships.

Max's Epoch (Stone Age Short)

Max wasn't born a prepper, he was forged into one.

(This short is exclusively available on MLBanner.com)

Hell's Requiem (03)

One man struggles to survive and find his way to a scientific sanctuary.

Time Slip (Stand Alone)

The time slip was his accident; can he use it to save the one he loves?

Cicada (04)

The scientific community of Cicada may be the world's only hope,

or it may lead to the end of everything.

Made in the USA
Middletown, DE
15 January 2024

47888402R00156